So this was like. . .

'Well, well, tl _____ the flesh,' Cr _____ sarcastic drawl, when his eyes had finished their exploration of her petite form. 'What the hell are you doing in the frozen north?'

He walked closer to her almost warily, like an animal stalking another, unknown species. 'And perhaps you'll tell me why you left Gresham in such a hurry, with scarcely a goodbye to anyone. . .certainly not to me. I've been burning to ask you that question for eight months. What do you have to say for yourself?'

Rebecca Lang trained to be a State Registered Nurse in Kent, England, where she was born. Her main focus of interest became operating theatre work, and she gained extensive experience in all types of surgery on both sides of the Atlantic. Now living in Toronto, Canada, she is married to a Canadian pathologist, and has three children. When not writing, Rebecca enjoys gardening, reading, theatre, exploring new places, and anything to do with the study of people.

Recent titles by the same author:

MIDNIGHT SUN

WEDDING SONG

BY
REBECCA LANG

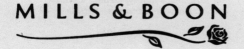

MILLS & BOON

MILLS & BOON, the Rose Device and
LOVE ON CALL *are trademarks of the publisher.*
Harlequin Mills & Boon Limited,
Eton House, 18-24 Paradise Road, Richmond, Surrey TW9 1SR
This edition published by arrangement with Harlequin Enterprises B.V.

© Rebecca Lang 1995

ISBN 0 263 79094 0

*Set in Times 10 on 11 pt. by
Rowland Phototypesetting Limited
Bury St Edmunds, Suffolk*

03-9506-51018

Made and printed in Great Britain

CHAPTER ONE

SHE had never seen so much snow. It had suddenly engulfed the airplane, like millions of goose feathers, as they had been coming in to land at Chalmers Bay, obscuring the view of the Arctic village that she had spotted briefly through the small window of the aircraft.

The landing had been more than a little bumpy. When there had been a spontaneous outburst of applause from the passengers she had known that she was finally in Chalmers Bay, in the Canadian Arctic, and she had looked around her a little sheepishly, hoping that she had not looked as raw as she felt. Not that she was raw, of course, having just spent six months virtually running a nursing station in a very remote place. She had simply come to an even more remote one, that was all.

Someone had rigged up a rope from the aircraft to the terminal building so that they could find their way. She had experienced 'white-outs' before at the nursing station in northern Manitoba, one of the Canadian provinces to the south, but nothing quite like this. And it was supposed to be coming up to spring here, too.

'Hang on to the rope, ma'am,' the steward had instructed her from the bottom of the steps, a blurred outline clothed in a heavy parka.

'Thank you,' she had said politely, wondering vaguely, as she had made her way tentatively over the snow, whether she indeed looked like a 'ma'am' rather than a 'miss' in her twenties.

Now she stood in the terminal building, the hood of

her parka pushed back, surrounded by her luggage, waiting patiently for someone from the Chalmers Bay medical station to meet her. There was no way anyone could drive through this. It was something she would have to get used to, since she was planning to be in Chalmers Bay for several weeks. The terminal building was small and utilitarian in the extreme, obviously not a place where people were expected to linger in comfort.

After about twenty minutes, which seemed interminable, a few individuals pushed their way in through the outside doors, battling against the wind, looking around for people they had come to meet. Meg watched hopefully. Then a woman came through, pushing back the snow-covered hood of her parka. She was young and attractive, a white woman with reddish hair. Meg felt a sense of relief, sure that this woman had come to get her. Probably she would be Dr Alanna Hargrove, who had already been working in Chalmers Bay for several weeks and was due to leave and go back down south very soon.

Apparently there were no permanent doctors in Chalmers Bay; they all worked on a short-term, rotating basis. There was a permanent nurse, so she had been told, by the name of Bonnie Mae, a young Canadian woman who came from the city of Edmonton, in the province of Alberta, which was hundreds of miles more or less directly to the south of where she was now.

'Meg Langham, I presume?' The young woman in the parka came forward, smiling, removing her gloves and holding out a welcoming hand. She had an English accent, like Meg's own, incongruous in this place.

'Yes.' Meg stepped forward.

'I'm Dr Hargrove, Alanna Hargrove. Welcome to Chalmers Bay.'

Meg relaxed, returning the smile and handshake. Again she felt renewed relief. Thank God she had been met by Dr Hargrove, and not. . .him.

'How was the flight?' Alanna Hargrove was even more attractive close up; her large hazel eyes under arched brows held a welcoming warmth. What would a woman like her be doing up here, in the isolation of the north? Meg found herself speculating. Maybe she was desperate for a job, just like me.

'It was a little rough,' she admitted. 'I'm certainly glad to be down, and to see you.'

'We'll put your luggage in the pick-up truck that I've got outside. This snow should be over in a few minutes; it's a sort of last effort of winter before the spring.' She laughed unconcernedly. 'Have you got gloves, Meg?'

'Yes.'

Between the two of them they humped her luggage outside to a battered blue pick-up truck. The cold, dry air set Meg's face tingling again, and she felt the mucous membranes of her nose stiffen with cold as she breathed. Very soon, she knew, the minute hairs inside her nostrils would get tiny balls of ice on them from frozen moisture, and her eyelashes would acquire a layer of frost. Snow danced around them, whipped by the wind.

'We'll wait it out in the cab of the truck. OK?' Alanna shouted above the wind.

The cab was relatively warm. Dr Hargrove started the engine and let it idle while they waited, so that a blast of hot air came from the heater to warm the enclosed space. It was a pity that Dr Hargrove was going to be leaving so soon, Meg felt, settling herself comfortably in the seat. They could most likely be good friends.

'You've worked for six months in northern Manitoba, I understand?' Dr Hargrove turned to her,

'All through the winter? So I guess you will have seen plenty of white-outs.'

'Quite a few,' Meg agreed modestly, 'I've got to the point where summer seems like a wonderful dream.'

'What made you come up here? I'm always curious to know why people come.'

'Well. . .' Meg was not quite ready for such direct-ness. 'To cut a long story short, I really needed a job. . .which was why I ended up in Manitoba in the first place. Coming up here seemed like the next step before trying to get back to so-called civilization. I lost my job in Gresham, Ontario, because of all the finan-cial cut-backs—the economy is really awful there—and someone told me about a job at the nursing station in northern Manitoba, so off I went.'

'You sound really adventurous, just the sort who's needed up here.'

'I'm not really. . .I just fell into it. Actually, I was wondering the same about you.'

'That's an even longer story,' Alanna smiled, a far-away look in her eyes briefly. 'I'll tell you about it before I leave Chalmers Bay.'

'Is he here?' Meg suddenly blurted out, unable to contain herself. 'I mean. . .Craig Russell?'

'Yes.' The other woman looked surprised. 'Dr Russell's been here for a week. Do you know him?'

'Er. . .yes. We worked together for several months in Gresham,' Meg answered, trying to keep her voice neutral.

'Oh? He didn't mention that he knew you.'

Several reasons occurred to Meg to account for why Craig Russell might have declined to mention that he knew her. One of them could be a guilty conscience. There couldn't be too many Meg Langhams around, even in this vast country.

'We worked in the operating-room together,' she

said. 'I was his scrub nurse for most of the time. He. . .
he used to tease me because I had to stand on a
stool. . .I'm so short compared with him.' She tried to
cover up.

'Do I detect some antipathy in your tone regarding
Dr Russell?' Alanna asked shrewdly. 'And I can see
why you needed a stool; you're very petite. . .five feet
two perhaps?'

'Yes. But I'm strong—tough as old nails, or whatever the saying is,' Meg said, thus circumventing the
question of her antipathy towards Craig Russell.

The swirling snow, encompassing them, had a mes-
merising effect; Meg let her thoughts float freely with
it. Had she known earlier that Craig Russell was going
to be here at Chalmers Bay, she certainly would not
have come, anxious though she had been for a job, she
told herself firmly. Yet would she. . .? An unexplained
providence had once again thrown them together in
this vast land, so that it seemed like an omen, a sum-
mons almost. From the time she had first seen him,
in the emergency department of the Gresham hospital,
she had felt drawn to him, as though there was a bond
between them that had always existed.

Fanciful thinking, she chided herself bitterly. Yet it
was there, dominating her life, not to be denied. As
it was, she had only known a week before her journey
up north that he was one of the doctors who would
be at the medical station—too late to back out of the
whole thing. Now she was stuck until the end of
August, which was when the weather changed rather
abruptly from summer to a brief autumn, followed
quickly by winter, passing from constant daylight to
constant darkness.

The Northern Medical Development Corps, with
headquarters in Toronto, and for whom she now
worked, knew better, apparently, than to ask people to

commit themselves definitely to more than six months maximum in the north, so they had employed her for the summer months only, after which she would again be jobless. Craig Russell, she assumed, would also go back to Gresham.

No, I would not have come had I known, she told herself sadly, even though I love him, so desperately that I will never get over him.

Before long the snow stopped abruptly, allowing them to move forward on to a snow-covered road that was only distinguishable because of tall poles in two rows bearing electricity cables. A world of white, mostly flat and barren, was revealed to Meg as she craned her neck to look all around her, the whiteness relieved by squat houses in the distance which were painted in pastel colours. As far as she could tell, they were made of wood, some clad with metal siding. Some were larger industrial buildings. The airstrip, with its terminal building, was situated at the extreme end of the village. Beyond it, Meg could see some large, dark outcrops of rock which looked stark against the vast sky that met the land at a far distant horizon.

The truck had huge, sturdy snow-tyres that helped the vehicle grip the ice beneath. There were no trees, and nothing green anywhere. Meg put on her dark glasses as a shaft of brilliant sunlight hit the road in front of them. On the northern side of the village was Coronation Gulf, a wide channel of sea that was part of the Arctic Ocean and which provided a lifeline to the community in the brief summer months when the ice temporarily retreated from the water long enough for ships and supply barges to get in.

'Call me Alanna,' Dr Hargrove said. 'We're all very informal up here. I'm sure you'll find that you get along quite well with Craig in this place; we're all sort of forced into a situation of intense co-operation. . .

it seems to come naturally after a day or two. . .so don't worry too much about that. Any mavericks don't last very long.'

'Thanks. . .'

'Craig has brought his small son up here to stay for a short while, by the way. They're living in town for the time being, with a woman friend of his who's in Chalmers Bay for a year to teach in the elementary school.'

'Really!' Meg exclaimed in a non-committal tone. 'I met his son once, actually.' Yes, there would be a woman somewhere on the scene, she thought. There always was with Craig Russell. . .or so she had heard. Even though one did not like to listen to rumours, it was impossible not to hear them in the somewhat insular environment of a hospital, where men and women were thrown together in a close working situation.

'When I leave Chalmers Bay,' Alanna was saying, 'Craig will be moving into the staff annexe with you. . . at least, when he's on call, which will be for quite a lot of the time. His son will of course stay with the schoolteacher, who has a child of her own about the same age.'

This verbal bombshell was delivered as they were bumping and slithering over a patch of rough ice, so that Meg had time to digest the information while she was bouncing about on the seat.

'You mean that he and I will actually be living together?' she queried disbelievingly.

'Well, sort of,' Alanna said gaily. 'Not to worry; there's plenty of privacy. You'll have your own bathroom.'

Meg was speechless, the breath knocked out of her as they went over a particularly vicious bump. There had been only one other wheeled vehicle on the road,

if it could be called that, while several skidoos careened
here and there around them in the soft snow, their
riders heavily swaddled in protective clothing. 'I
see. . .' she said at last, swallowing a nervous lump in
her throat.

'I'll drive you straight to the staff annexe, show you
around quickly,' Alanna explained. 'Then I must leave
you for a while because we've got something scheduled
for a bit later on. So you just relax, make yourself at
home. There's a meal waiting for you. Either later this
evening or tomorrow I'll show you around the medical
station. . .or Bonnie Mae will. Bonnie has her own
quarters.' She did not say when Meg would meet Dr
Craig Russell. 'We have one other full-time person
here—Skip, the operating-room technician. I guess
you know that, since you'll be doing some of his work
when he has to go down to Edmonton for that refresher
course.'

'Yes, that was part of the arrangement.'

'You're a fully registered nurse, of course?'

'Yes.'

The staff annexe at the medical station proved to be
more spacious and comfortable than she had expected,
with a large, cosy living-cum-dining-room which at first
glance showed all the gadgetry and modern con-
veniences of a home down south. No doubt Alanna
Hargrove had added the colourful, feminine touches
that made the room welcoming. In addition, there was
a kitchen and small laundry-room, again with all the
latest gadgetry, and there were two bedrooms, divided
by a narrow passage.

'I'll make you tea,' Alanna announced when they
had deposited Meg's luggage in one of the bedrooms.
'Get yourself settled in, then I'll see you later. That's
my room opposite.'

'Thanks, Alanna. I appreciate having someone here to show me around.'

The whole building was a metal-clad portable, well-insulated against the cold. Her room had a tiny, triple-glazed window with a thermal shade. Meg looked at the bed, with its thick duvet and blankets, and the small *en-suite* bathroom. She was certainly not going to have to rough it.

'Here you are, Meg.' Alanna handed her a mug of hot tea in the sitting-room, after rushing around quickly to make it. 'Now don't forget that we're all on a first-name basis here. If Craig gives you any trouble, which I doubt, you just tell me. . .I'll sort it out before I leave here.'

Feeling most of her previous tension drain from her as she sipped the tea, Meg nodded.

'Since today's Saturday,' Alanna said, gulping the last of her tea, 'you won't be officially on duty until Monday, but we'll use what's left of the weekend to orientate you to the medical station and to the town itself, if there's time. OK?'

'Yes. . .OK. Thanks.'

'I must fly. They'll be gnashing their teeth over there and pacing the floor, waiting for me.' Before she went, she flung open the door of an ice-box to indicate two covered dishes inside. 'This is your meal, Meg. Just put it in the microwave oven for a few minutes. OK?'

'I'll do that, Alanna. Don't worry about me. After northern Manitoba I can survive anything, believe me!' Meg smiled. Dr Hargrove had certainly picked up the North American habit of saying 'OK' in every conceivable context. It was definitely a useful word.

'I'll try to remember that you're tough, in spite of that very fragile appearance. Bye!'

Then Meg was alone in the quiet annexe, with only a faint, distant roaring of wind as it blew over the open

tundra and encountered the obstacles of the spread-out
buildings of the medical station, which was at the other
end of the village from the airstrip. With mug in hand,
she stood in the centre of the sitting-room, letting her
eyes rove slowly over the bookcases, the television and
VCR, over framed prints on the walls, over the bright
cushions.

Sitting down in a comfortable chair, she relaxed
back, closing her eyes. It felt good to have successfully
completed a six-month locum contract at a nursing
station in a remote area where there were no doctors,
where she had had no one to rely on but herself in
making decisions, as it now felt good to be settled
again in a job that could be even more interesting,
challenging in a somewhat different way.

Inevitably, as it always did in quiet moments, in spite
of her best efforts to concentrate on something else,
her mind wandered back to the time when she had
first set eyes on Dr Craig Russell, about one year and
three months ago. . .

She had been relatively new to this country then,
only able to get in because her parents had brought
her and her sister to Canada when she was a baby,
having stayed long enough to get citizenship for the
whole family, then deciding to go back to England.

When she had returned to this country as a young
trained nurse she had been eager to impress, to fit in
at the big impersonal hospital where the other nurses
had seemed, without exception, so confident, so sure
of themselves and everything else, many of them
aggressive to the point of perpetual bossiness. For the
purposes of self-preservation, she had tried to emulate
them, to cultivate a veneer of invulnerability, even
though it went against the grain with her. She was not
naturally a bossy or pushy person, or prone to hiding
her real feelings.

It was only after she had been at the hospital for a few weeks that it had gradually begun to dawn on her that the others were not as confident, as knowledgeable, as they seemed; with many it was an act, a tough exterior to hide a human, weak interior which it was not the done thing to exhibit. Exploit or be exploited, that seemed to be the common unspoken motto; look for the weaknesses in others, but never expose your own. It had all been a big eye-opener to her, who had never before worked in such a viciously competitive atmosphere where professionals were competing openly for jobs that were slowly but inexorably drying up at all levels in the general economic recession.

Meg had been made to feel that as a foreigner, clearly defined by her accent, she had been lucky to get a job. . .more telling on her because she knew it was true, which had nothing to do with her professional competence.

None the less, she had gradually relaxed and gained confidence in that boiler-house atmosphere, because she had come to realise that she was good at her job, well-trained. She had encountered nothing that she did not know how to deal with in the busy emergency department where she had first been put to work as a new employee at University Hospital in Gresham, while she was waiting for a promised position in the huge operating suite, operating being her main area of expertise.

It was in the emergency department late one evening that she had first met Craig Russell's son, then Dr Russell himself, without knowing at the time that he was a doctor at the hospital, or realising that later she would be working very closely with him in the operating-rooms.

Now, thinking about it, her cheeks warmed with the memory of how she had made a fool of herself with

him, because she had wanted to present that blasé
quality to the world that she saw all around her. It
was after that incident that she had decided just to be
herself. . .the quietly competent Meg Langham, up
front, no pretence, no jargon.

The boy had been brought into the emergency
department by his grandmother, who, it had turned
out, was an Englishwoman who had lived in Canada
for many years. It was wintertime and the boy, seven
years old, had fallen off a sled earlier in the day and
broken his arm. The fracture, a greenstick fracture,
common in children, had gone undetected until the
late evening when the boy had complained of persistent
pain in the arm that seemed to be from more than the
bruising sustained in the fall.

He was a sweet boy, fair-haired, blue-eyed, who was
trying very hard to be brave, not to cry. Meg had been
very gentle with him, had put him on a stretcher in
one of the many examination cubicles, his grandmother
sitting by his side. Meg had smiled reassuringly, gently
easing off the large square silk scarf that had been tied
as a sling to support the injured arm. 'Show me exactly
where it hurts, Rob. We'll be very careful,' she had
told him.

'It's right here.' Rob, his voice wobbly with the effort
not to cry, had indicated a spot on his upper left arm
that Meg could see was bruised and swollen.

'Mmm. . .yes,' she had murmured. 'I'm going to put
a bandage round that, Rob, just to support it, then
I'm going to get a doctor to see you. We'll get an
X-ray done. Ever had an X-ray before?'

'No. Does it hurt?'

'No, it's just a sort of photograph,' she assured him.

'A fractured humerus?' Rob's grandmother queried.
'I blame myself for not noticing it earlier, the poor
boy. I just thought it was bruised. . .'

'Don't blame yourself,' Meg said, busily filling in an X-ray request form. 'These fractures in young children are often not complete breaks, as you may know, so they're not always easy to detect without an X-ray. Children's bones are so flexible that they often just bend and splinter a bit. . .like a green stick, in fact.'

After she had put a quick call through to the orthopaedic resident-in-training who was on call for the night, since by then it was eleven p.m., she gently put a support bandage around the area of the fracture and put the arm back into the sling. 'That bandage will support the fracture, if there is one, and help keep the swelling down. I don't think there's much bleeding,' she explained to the grandmother. 'His pulse is quite steady.'

'Thank you, Nurse. I feel better now that we're actually here.'

'Good. Now, Rob, have you got any other aches and pains? Did you hit your head when you fell? Look up to the ceiling, I want to shine a light in your eyes.'

'I didn't hit my head,' Rob said, becoming more confident. 'The snow was really thick there, real soft, so my head just went into it.'

Ten minutes later the orthopaedic resident arrived, breathlessly. His name was Dr Becker, a skinny young man, with heavy glasses that made him look like an owl, and a shock of mousy hair that was always untidy. The orthopaedic service was one of the busiest in University Hospital, causing Dr Becker to be in an almost permanent state of rush. Now he came into the cubicle, his none too clean white coat flapping open over a crumpled green scrub suit, the pockets heavily weighed down with a stethoscope, an auroscope, various notebooks, pens and small pads of paper.

'Hi, Meg,' he said with an exaggerated, resigned

bonhomie as he bounded to a halt beside the stretcher.
'What have we got here, then?'

Meg explained.

'Hi there, Rob. . .hi.' Richard Becker's tired smile
encompassed Rob and his grandmother. 'Better get
the X-ray guy to come here with the portable, Meg,
instead of going up to X-Ray with the stretcher; he
was just here, taking some pictures of another of my
patients.'

'Yes, he's on his way. You just have to affix your
signature to the form.'

'Sure!' With a flourish, he extracted one of his many
pens from a sagging pocket. 'Then we'll get down to
the nitty gritty. It's going to be one of those nights, I
can tell. . .by the itching of my thumbs. . .or is it
palms? Anyway, the other guy I'm looking at broke his
arm too—fell off a motorbike while it was stationary.
Would you believe it? I hate to think what he would
have done to himself if he was moving.' He rolled his
eyes, smiling at Rob, who allowed himself a little grin
in return. 'So you see, fella, your injury ain't so bad
after all.'

Fifteen minutes later they were standing in one of
the small staff offices in the clinical area looking at
the boy's X-rays displayed on the lighted wall panel.
Dr Becker had a comradely arm around Meg's shoulders as they looked at the films together.

'Let me lean on you, Meg,' Richard said, 'otherwise
I'm liable to fall over from fatigue. . . Can't remember
when I last had a decent sleep.' He leaned against her
in mock-collapse. 'I'm running on adrenalin.'

'At least this is straightforward,' Meg said brightly.
'A simple splint and sling should suffice for now, don't
you think?'

'Yeah. . .' he agreed, peering owlishly. 'I'll slap that
on in no time. First of all, I want to put a plaster of

Paris on that motorbike guy. Can you help me with that? What a life this is, eh, Meg? At least you're officially off duty in a few minutes. I've got to go on all night.'

'You love it,' she chided him. 'It makes you feel wanted.'

'Maybe,' he grinned, giving her a playful peck on the cheek. 'That's not always enough compensation for no love life, no sex life and not much sleep.'

'Richard!' she exclaimed in mock-horror. 'No talk like that on the job! I'll get the plaster cart organised, so you get yourself kitted out with that plastic apron and overshoes.'

'OK, boss! You don't fancy being my love life, do you, honey?'

'No, I don't,' she laughed as he turned his eyes mournfully upon her. 'I've already got my hands full in that department.' That wasn't altogether true, but no matter.

'I bet you have!' A deep voice, heavy with sarcasm, came from behind them. Meg turned quickly to see a man standing in the doorway, a cynical expression on his face. He could have been there for some time. 'Better get your hands full in this department. I'm Rob's father.'

Richard Becker turned casually, running a hand through his already tousled hair. 'Oh, hi there,' he said cheerfully. Meg admired his ease. Nothing ever fazed Richard. 'I'm Dr Becker. You'll be pleased to know that your son has a very mild fracture of the left humerus. We'll put a splint on and he can go home right away. Kids' bones heal up very quickly without much in the way of treatment. We'll give him an appointment to see an orthopaedic surgeon in a couple of days. In the meantime, just get him to rest the limb as much as possible, give him some analgesic for pain if necessary. Take a look at the X-rays.' He swung his arm in a magnanimous arc to encompass the displayed films.

'I already did,' the stranger said curtly from the doorway. He was tall and broad, athletic-looking, with penetrating blue eyes that did not smile, and dark, longish hair. A heavy winter jacket made him seem even bigger, somehow threatening. Meg could not associate him with the pale, fair boy on the stretcher, who she felt instinctively would be gentle by nature. Still, one could not always go by superficial appearances.

'Have you seen your son?' she asked, trying to control the colour that was creeping into her cheeks, hoping this man realised that such *badinage* between doctors and nurses meant nothing; it merely helped them to survive.

'Yes,' he said. 'I came here as quickly as I could. I've only just heard about the accident; I've been out of town for two days. I hate it when things like this happen while I'm away; it could have been very serious.'

'Yes,' she agreed, 'but these things happen, however careful one is.' While they had been talking, Meg had quickly checked the stainless-steel cart that was kept in the room, which held the rolls of plaster of Paris, as well as all the other accoutrements for putting a plaster cast on a limb. She began to push it towards the door. 'Come with me,' she invited crisply. 'Perhaps you would like to stay with your son while Dr Becker puts a plaster on another patient. . .that won't take long. . .then maybe you would like to watch while he puts a splint on Rob.'

'Mmm. . .' he said, looking at her levelly, an odd glint of amusement in his eyes, making Meg feel momentarily gauche and susceptible to the quiet masculinity that he exuded, dominating the confined space. Quickly she pushed the cart along the corridor to the cubicle where the young owner of the motorbike lay, aware of the man following behind her, aware of his eyes on her.

'Perhaps you'd like to sit with your son, Mr Juneau,' she offered, trying to look and sound the epitome of efficiency.

'I'll stand, thank you,' he said. 'And my name's Russell. . .Craig Russell. . . I have a different name from my son.'

'Oh, I see,' she said. She did not see, but it didn't matter. There could be a number of reasons why the names were different.

While he paced the corridor with a certain impatience, Meg pulled the cubicle curtain to shut him out and turned her attention to the young man who lay waiting rather sheepishly, watched by his equally silent girlfriend who was clothed in black leather. Richard Becker started a verbal patter as he went about the business of applying a plaster of Paris, at which he was an expert.

In no time at all they were back with Rob, splinting his arm, while his father stood in the doorway watching. Meg chatted to Rob to keep his mind on positive things. 'Which hand do you write with, Rob?' she asked.

Rob visibly brightened, obviously thinking about certain possibilities for the first time. 'My right hand. Gee, maybe I can call in sick for the French test next week!'

'It's your left arm, Rob,' his father's deep voice commented from just behind Meg, making her tinglingly aware of his presence.

'Oh, yeah. . .' Rob conceded thoughtfully. 'I bet Madame Fricke doesn't know what hand I write with.'

'She will when I tell her,' his dad grinned, coming forward to stand by the stretcher next to Meg so that she was wedged between him and Richard. Dr Becker was like a sweet, playful puppy compared with the rather brooding man who was the boy's father, who seemed to miss nothing. 'If I don't tell her, Granny will,' he continued. 'That's a promise.'

'You meany!' His son smiled back; he obviously had a good, close relationship with his father. 'Did you bring me back that T-shirt you promised to get me in Boston, Dad?'

'Sure did! I had a hard time locating it, though, so I shall expect abject gratitude and no more demands for the next few weeks.'

'Great!' The small boy relaxed back against his pillows, satisfied.

Where was the mother? Meg wondered. There was no mention of her. The boy had a slightly lost, forlorn air, she thought, even though it was apparent that both his father and granny adored him. They watched him closely, their eyes warm with affection, tinged with anxiety.

When Meg left the cubicle to look in the appointment book for the orthopaedic clinic, Mr Russell followed her. 'Could you bring your son back on this day to see Dr Gregson, the orthopaedic surgeon, in Outpatients?' She handed him a card with a time on it. 'Is that a convenient time for you? I could possibly make it to coincide with the French test,' she added mischievously.

'My son would love you forever,' Mr Russell said, looking at the card. The remark, which normally would have sounded routine, trite, seemed to Meg to be oddly personal coming from this man. For a few seconds she had a nostalgic wish that the boy would love her, as though he were a long-lost son of her own.

'I'd prefer to see Dr Campion instead, if that's no problem for you,' he added, handing back the card. 'I know Dr Campion quite well, and so does Rob.'

'Um. . .yes. I'll just have to change the day, that's all. They come on alternate days.' It did not seem unusual that he would know Dr Campion.

'Hope it's not an imposition, Miss—er——?' the drawling voice spoke just behind her as she bent over the appointment book.

'Oh, no. . .' Meg straightened up to hand him a new card, her eyes meeting his at close quarters. She stood as though transfixed while his perceptive gaze moved over her features, lingering on her mouth. His observation was not calculated; she had the very odd feeling that he could not help himself, that he was attracted to her, and the thought warmed her in a way that was equally odd. It was not as though she didn't have men friends and was thus overly susceptible to a good-looking man. . . She had several at the present time.

'Considerate of you, Miss—er——?'

'Not at all,' she said, hiding behind the safety of her professional voice, her English accent very pronounced, contrasting with his North American drawl. That English grandmother, she suddenly thought, must be his mother, since she was Mrs Russell. 'It's all part of the job.'

'Miss. . .?' he persisted.

'Miss Langham,' she said. 'Meg Langham.'

'Thank you, Miss Langham,' he said, taking the new card. 'And thank you for being so charming to my son. Hospitals are such intimidating places, plus the fact that I get so uptight when anything happens to him. It's always a major catastrophe when it's your own child.'

'Yes. . .not to worry,' she said, smiling at him as airily as she could. 'Perhaps you've been watching too much TV. Those medical shows aren't necessarily true to life. They're somewhat—er—corny, and the drama of real life in a hospital doesn't generally involve all those frantic, constant crises. . .sirens screaming. . . you know, all that tight-lipped, flinty-eyed, terse dialogue stuff.'

'Is that so?' he said slowly, looking at her from under lowered brows as he stroked his chin thoughtfully.

'Yes,' she said emphatically.

'I'll bear that in mind. . .definitely,' he said.

It was well beyond midnight, over half an hour since her shift had ended and the night staff had appeared to take over, when she finally waved goodbye to Rob and his family. She had chosen to see the case through to its conclusion before going off duty.

'Goodbye, Rob; you've been very brave,' she said. 'Come in to see me if I'm still here when you come to Outpatients.'

'Why wouldn't you be here?' the boy enquired curiously.

'I expect to be working in the operating-rooms soon,' she confided. 'Hope I don't see you there.'

'One never knows,' Rob's father murmured. 'Goodnight, Miss Langham. Thanks again.'

Before they had gone more than a few yards down the corridor, Dr Becker came out of the treatment cubicle, struggling into his white coat.

'Hey, Meg!' he said in a loud, jovial voice. 'Thanks for your expert ministrations, as always, and goodnight.'

'Goodnight, Richard,' she said resignedly, not looking at the departing trio.

Three weeks later she got the job she wanted in the huge suite that held at least twenty-five operating-rooms. On the first day there, in the ordered hustle and bustle, among the milling human bodies both upright and supine in the corridors that connected the rooms, she felt like a very small cog in a giant machine. After a two-week orientation period, after which she knew her way around superficially, she was detailed to work in the plastic surgery service, one of the slower-paced, less frenetic services.

It was during that third week that she came face to face with Rob's father in the OR corridor. . .wearing a scrub suit and a cotton scrub cap. He was with another man, identically attired. While she stared, open-mouthed, wondering whether he would recognise her, he looked at her, then took one of the disposable face masks from a box above the scrub sinks outside the room where she was to work and tied it over his nose and mouth. Then he turned to her and gave her a considered stare, then a slow wink, before disappearing with his colleague into the room where she was working.

With a fast-beating heart and a dawning realisation, she quickly consulted a copy of the long operating list for the day that was posted on the wall by the door of the plastic surgery suite. Dr Alexander C. Russell was one of the plastic surgeons operating that day, and she would be scrubbing for two of his small cases initially, then two of his longer cases after that. When she had looked at the list earlier, she had not made the connection. Russell was a fairly common name, after all.

One of the other nurses came up to read the list over her shoulder. 'Gee, you're lucky to be scrubbing with Dr Russell—he's gorgeous!' she enthused enviously. 'A great surgeon too. He really takes time to explain what he's doing, to talk to you, you know.'

Meg did not feel lucky, she felt sick. She recalled the sound of her voice in the emergency department, prissily enunciating, 'Perhaps you've been watching too

much TV. . .' Then she had said something about the
drama of real life. . .

'Oh, hell. . .hell,' she muttered. Now she had to
scrub for him, to pretend that she had not said those
patronising things. It was doubtful that he had
forgotten. . .

Meg got up stiffly from the chair in the staff annexe
at Chalmers Bay medical station, bringing her thoughts
abruptly back to the present. A lot of water had flowed
under the bridge since her first days in University
Hospital's operating-rooms. Now here she was in the
Arctic, about to work again with Alexander Craig
Russell. . .by accident or uncanny fate rather than by
design.

From the ice-box in the small kitchen she took out
the two dishes that contained her meal, one of meat
and vegetables, the other a fruit pie, already cooked.
After putting them in the microwave oven, she set the
timer. As she waited she explored again. There was a
radio telephone, plus other telephones for local use.
She assumed that satellites facilitated modern communication systems.

Footsteps sounded on the wooden floor of the
covered way leading from the staff annexe to the medical station, which she had noted when she had come
in. The outer storm door opened, then the inner door.
Meg turned, expecting Alanna Hargrove. . .

CHAPTER TWO

CRAIG RUSSELL came in, a commanding presence, making the room seem instantly smaller. The sight of him, when he had been so vividly in her thoughts a few seconds ago, rendered her virtually paralysed with a fearful anticipation, as though she had found herself abruptly on stage in a play for which she had never seen the script, where fantasy and reality mingled in a frightening maelstrom of emotion. So this was what stage fright was like. . .this inability to utter, to think, to move.

He wore a bulky, padded jacket, checked red and black, over a scrub suit. Apart from that, he looked about the same—longish thick hair that curled slightly, intent blue eyes, firm, lean features, an air of quiet intelligence and compassion, a brooding, intense quality in his regard. . .not that he looked particularly compassionate where she was concerned as his shrewd eyes encountered her own.

Abruptly he came to a halt a few feet away from her. It was about eight months since she had last seen him. Now, as they looked at each other silently for long seconds, in which time seemed to be suspended, she wanted to rush forward and fling her arms around him, like a lover.

From the very beginning, she admitted now, she had had a 'thing' for him, born of a mutual attraction, when she had just known him as Rob's father. He must never know now how much she still cared for him. Lusting after Craig Russell was pretty hopeless, so she had heard, unless that was only what one wanted in return. . .lust. Subsequent experience, although brief, had confirmed the rumour. Apparently, his motto was 'love 'em and leave 'em'. The love of his life, according to that same rumour, had been the mother of his son.

'Well, well, the elusive Meg Langham in the flesh,' he said at last, his voice a sarcastic drawl, when his eyes had finished their exploration of her petite form which was still clad in the comfortable leggings and sweater that she had worn for travel. 'What the hell are you doing in the frozen north?'

He walked closer to her almost warily, like an animal stalking another, unknown species. 'And perhaps you'll tell me why you left Gresham in such a hurry, with scarcely a goodbye to anyone. . .certainly not to me. I've been burning to ask you that question for eight months. What do you have to say for yourself?'

As he spoke he shrugged out of his heavy jacket and advanced into the room as though he had every right to be there, which she supposed he had. She watched the familiar ripple of his firm muscled arms, the powerful body under the thin fabric of the scrub suit. Hungrily she renewed her visual acquaintance with his physical being, her senses devouring him as though she had been starving for him. Aware of her appraisal, there was a stillness in him as he met her regard.

Meg found her voice. 'Well, I might ask the same. . . What are you doing here?'

'Oh, I've been here before, several times. . .not actually to the Northwest Territories; this is the first time. I usually go to the Yukon. . .doing my bit for the country, you might say, sharing my surgical expertise where it's most needed, and all that, for a couple of months each year or whatever.' There was a self-deprecating tone in his voice. Even though he expected her to explain herself, he clearly did not want to give an account of himself to her. 'I'm talking about you. . . you!' There was barely controlled anger in him now as he confronted her, his face pale and taut.

Meg ran her tongue over her dry lips, not knowing how to answer him. How could one explain adequately a fear of being hurt to the one who would be the cause of that hurt? Involuntarily she looked him over again, familiar in the garb of his profession, and she remembered the feel of his bare skin, warm against her own in other surroundings, in the secret, velvety nights of hot summer. . .

From experience she knew that he seldom talked about himself or his private life to colleagues; there was still so much that she didn't know, perhaps would never know now. Probably if she had not actually met his son she would never have known that he had one. Had there been time, he might have divulged more of himself to her.

'So what about Gresham, Miss Langham?' he persisted coldly.

'I was terminated, as you must surely know,' she said in a hollow, level tone, while inwardly she was in a turmoil, the humiliation of her past experience coming back to her. 'At the time, I thought that perhaps you had something to do with it. . .and you were conveniently out of the way when it happened, for three weeks.'

'Why would I have had anything to do with it?' His voice, terse and cold, cut right through her emotional armour. 'I heard later that you'd been laid off, together with a number of other people, that you'd already left town. No forwarding address. No nothing! I could have offered you a job at my private clinic, the Gresham clinic, if I'd known you were in dire straits.' As he spoke, his eyes continued to roam over her, a cynical curl to his lips, so that it was impossible for Meg to tell how he felt about seeing her again. Not exactly ecstatic, she observed soberly.

'Well, you didn't,' she said, trying to keep a threatening tremble out of her voice.

'How could I? Why the hell didn't you wait until I got back from the States? You had gone by the time I got back,' he said, looking at her assessingly, with a hard anger. 'You could have had the decency, the good manners, to let me know why you were leaving the city.' He looked at her soft blonde hair which fell in a profusion of loose, untidy curls to just above her shoulders. She knew that it framed her delicate, heart-shaped face in such a way that she appeared deceptively childlike, in need of protection. Where he was concerned, she was certainly vulnerable.

'I had been under the impression that we had something going for us, something good that could have gone on being good. I don't like women walking out on me,' he said harshly.

'I bet you don't,' she said, gaining courage from desperation. 'You like to do the walking out, so I've heard.'

'You listen to gossip, do you? Then you act on it? How very naïve!' His hands were clenched at his sides; his lips, which had so long ago kissed her with abandoned passion, were compressed into a line of contempt. 'I thought you were different from all the others. Less bitchy. It seems I was pretty naïve myself.'

'I am different!' Meg felt tears prick her eyes. Although she had anticipated a difficult encounter, it was all going hideously wrong. 'But you're not!'

She thought he might hit her as he came over to stand inches away from her. 'What the hell do you know about me?'

I know that you're a good surgeon, a good

doctor. . .I know what you're like as a lover. The words were spoken in Meg's head, the inner voice that did not lie. . .I know that I could not bear to be less than everything to you. . .not for long, anyway. Because I love you. . .

'Enough, I think,' she said bravely. 'It wouldn't have worked anyway. I think I would have been too. . .too possessive. As for your involvement in my being "let go", as the saying is, one of the reasons could have been the time you. . .you kissed me in the prep-room in the OR. The head nurse saw you. . .'

Meg knew it sounded lame, yet at the time, when Craig had come up behind her, kissed her on the back of the neck and run his hands briefly over her breasts when he had thought they had been alone, she had been aware that they had been observed. He had ignored her hastily whispered protest to be careful. In the operating-room one did not cross the sometimes fine line between professionalism and one's personal considerations. Normally, he had been the epitome of decorum; it was almost as though he had wanted to precipitate something. . .

When he had gone she had seen the head nurse watching her; there had been a look of shocked surprise in her superior's expression, and something else. . . Jealousy.

'I've kissed nurses before in the prep-room. . .not very often, I'll admit. I doubt that Joyce Travers would hold it against me, or you.' There was a note of incredulity in his voice.

'Not you! Me definitely,' she said.

Just then the internal telephone rang, making Meg jump. Craig Russell strode over to the instrument, which was on top of a bookcase. There was an easy familiarity about everything he did, once again as though he had a right. Would he, she wondered, feel he had a right to come into her bedroom when he moved into the annexe?

After a brief conversation he turned back to her. 'We have another case to do over there in a short while—an emergency. They want to know if you could help; we're going to need all the help we can get.'

'Well, yes, of course.'

'I know you haven't eaten or had much of a chance to rest. Have your dinner, don't rush it, then come on over,' Craig said, immediately reverting to a professional alertness. Picking up his coat, he shrugged into it. 'Welcome to Chalmers Bay, Meg,' he added with irony.

Then he was gone, the door slamming behind him hollowly. Through a small glass pane she watched him walk away from her when she wanted to call out to him, to call him back to her so that things could be as they had been during the summer that she remembered so vividly.

She forced herself into a state of calm as she ate her meal at the table. Perhaps it was just as well that she would not have time to think too much before starting work. Just as she was finishing, footsteps in the covered way made her look up nervously, holding her breath in anticipation of another verbal onslaught.

A woman of remarkable appearance squeezed her way into the room through the narrow door. Tall and very large, she advanced into the room like a battleship in full sail.

'Hi! I'm Bonnie Mae, the permanent nurse in this place.' She came towards Meg with a rolling walk to accommodate her massive thighs. She was clothed in a pale yellow trouser suit, cut like a scrub suit, with a loose, voluminous top, and her hair was covered with a blue cotton scrub cap. There was a red stethoscope hanging round her neck.

The hand that she held out to Meg was surprisingly small and dainty compared with her large, capable-looking arms. 'Just thought I'd come over quickly to say hello before we get moving with this case. Sure pleased to see you!' She had a drawling Canadian accent.

Meg got to her feet and took the hand. Bonnie Mae was what her male colleagues at Gresham would have called well-stacked. 'Hello,' she smiled. 'I'm Meg.'

'I'll take you back over with me and show you where to change, Meg. We have a guy over there who was attacked by a grizzly out in the sticks. He's a real mess. They brought him up here 'cos it was closer than Yellowknife. It's great to have you here. . .real great!'

Later, Meg glanced at the clock in the medical station operating-room that was now becoming familiar to her and could hardly believe that so much time had passed already since they had made a start. Her tiredness from the journey was pushed aside as she concentrated on the job for which she was trained, in which she had much experience.

Blood dripped swiftly, drop by measured drop, from the plastic bag hanging on the metal pole, into the drip-chamber of the intravenous tubing. She watched the drops with a professional eye, calculating from long experience how fast they were moving per minute, manipulating the small valve on the tubing with her fingers to speed up the flow a little as the blood ran down the tubing into a vein in her patient's neck, his limbs being out of commission. Then she turned to the anaesthetic machine, her eyes going swiftly over the gauges that informed her of the amounts of oxygen and nitrous oxide that were flowing into her patient's lungs. Automatically her eyes moved on to the blood-pressure, pulse, and temperature monitor, with its electronic graph and digital numbers a bright green against a screen of darker colour, then on to the pulse-oxymetre screen, its numbers red, which told her how much circulating oxygen was in his bloodstream.

She made a few notes on the anaesthetic chart, before her observations began again. Now and then one of the monitors pinged or clicked rapidly, spewing out a printed electrocardiograph, to break the near silence in the operating-room, together with the muted whooshing and sighing sound of the automatic respirator. It was only a light anaesthetic, just enough to keep the patient under while the two surgeons worked on him. It was going to take a long time. . .

Meg felt confident that she could go into any operating-room in the world and know what to do; and it didn't matter at the moment that she was having to work with a man about whom she felt very ambivalent. There was a strange *déjà vu* feeling as she glanced briefly at Craig Russell's bent head, and thought again of the mysterious fate that had manipulated both their lives so that, against all odds, their paths had crossed once again. . .

'You OK, Meg?' Bonnie Mae, who was the circulating nurse, had come up to her to whisper the question in her ear.

Meg nodded, smiling. It was already evident that they were going to be friends. Bonnie Mae knew the community, the surrounding area and the mines, whose workers they serviced, like nobody else. She was evidently very experienced and competent.

'You get to be everything up here in the Arctic,' Bonnie Mae said in a stage whisper, 'including an anaesthetist. But don't expect to get paid any extra for it!' They chuckled together, standing at the head of the operating table in a stance of easy camaraderie.

'That must have been some grizzly, eh?' Bonnie Mae

continued with awe in her voice, her eyes going over
the body of their patient on the operating table.

'Yes,' Meg agreed feelingly. 'It was lucky there was
someone else around. . .the bush plane.'

The man lay stretched out, covered and wrapped
with sterile drapes which left his four limbs exposed.
His arms were out on arm-boards, at right angles to
his body, the extensive wounds that had recently been
cleaned and sutured now covered with sterile gauze.
He was lying on a heating pad through which hot water
flowed from a machine, to minimise shock. Both surgeons now worked on the legs, one each, carefully,
painstakingly debriding, cleaning and suturing the
awful wounds, inserting small plastic drainage tubes
here and there.

Meg averted her eyes, dwelling on the seeming
miracle of the passing bush plane whose pilot had witnessed the attack by the grizzly bear on John Oldman,
an Indian trapper working in a remote area. The bear,
recently woken from its winter hibernation, hungry and
irritable, had attacked without obvious provocation.
The pilot had buzzed the scene, flying as low as he
dared, and had managed to frighten off the bear long
enough for him to look for a place to land near by
and find his way back in time to the injured man.

Even though he had been wearing thick clothing,
John Oldman's limbs had been flayed by the deadly
curved claws of the bear, in some places right to the
bone, strips of skin and muscle peeled back. Conse-
quently he had lost a lot of blood. The bush pilot had
rendered first aid as best he could, then had decided
to fly the injured man north to the Chalmers Bay
medical station, which was closer than the city of
Yellowknife to the south, the capital of the vast and
very sparsely populated Northwest Territories. Also he
would have had to waste time stopping at remote

weather stations to refuel. There were huge areas in the Territories where there were no people, no help or habitation.

There was a certain tension in the room as each staff member concentrated on the task in hand, giving their best. For Meg's part, she felt a tightness in her throat, an ever-present anxiety that she had learned to live with when faced with accident victims. In her considered opinion, John Oldman would pull through, but they were not yet out of the woods by any means. Severe shock could kill. As for the actual wounds, it was a good thing that Craig Russell was a plastic surgeon, and a very good one at that. His expertise would lessen the amount of work that would have to be done later, re-suturing wounds that did not heal well, removing unsightly scars.

As though she had sent him a telepathic message, he became aware of her scrutiny and looked up, his perceptive eyes looking disconcertingly into hers. She felt her own eyes widen for an unguarded moment, her lips part under the covering face mask in expectation of having to make a witty rejoinder to some succinct remark of his. That was how it had been at University Hospital. Then it would be just like the old days, almost. . .like the old days when she had trusted him.

This time he did not joke. He paused to stretch tired shoulder muscles, tilting his head back, moving it slowly from side to side. Meg could almost feel the ache herself, could feel the tiredness of his eyes. After all, she knew the feeling well.

'Take a little breather, Alanna.' Craig looked at Dr Hargrove who stood on the opposite side of the operating table.

A tinge of something like envy assailed Meg as she saw Craig turn his considerable charm on Alanna, even though she knew that Alanna had recently been married to another doctor who had worked at Chalmers Bay and would not be the slightest bit affected, as she was, by such attention. The new husband, so Bonnie Mae had informed her, was a Dr Owen Bentall who had left for British Columbia when Craig had arrived to take his place. When Alanna went also, they would be getting a second doctor whose name she did not yet know.

'If I take a breather, Craig, it's going to be for a cup of tea,' Alanna said emphatically. 'Otherwise I'm sure I'll fall asleep on the spot if I dare break my concentration. Do you realize we've been at this. . .' she glanced quickly at the wall clock '. . .for three and a half hours?'

'Yeah. . .' Craig arched his back tiredly. 'Feels like it. We'll take a tea-break; we'll take turns. How about it, Bonnie Mae?'

'Sure, Doc!' Bonnie Mae agreed, turning her vast bulk towards them, resplendent in her yellow outfit. She had been adding notes to the patient's chart at a side-table and weighing the blood-soaked sponges in order to get a reasonably accurate tally of the blood loss. 'Sure, I'll make tea. I reckon the nurses should have it first.'

'I agree with that.' Alanna turned to smile at Meg. 'Especially since Meg here is doing double duty, doing my job as well as her own. How's the blood-pressure, Meg?'

'It's one-fifteen over sixty-five,' Meg answered. 'Everything's stable. Oxygen level ninety-eight per cent.'

'Good.'

In truth, Meg felt she wasn't really doing much. All she had to do was watch the monitors that were programmed to sound the alarm with the slightest irregularity in the patient's condition. Alanna had

induced the patient, put him to sleep. In this emergency, when both doctors were occupied in stopping
the bleeding, she had been detailed to act as ongoing
anaesthetist.

It was important that blood did not leak out as fast
as it was put in. Their supply of blood was limited.
They had telephoned to the city for more, to come up
on the next available plane.

'OK, you guys,' Bonnie Mae announced jovially.
'I'm going out to the office to make and drink tea.
Anything you desperately want before I go? I don't
want you bawling after me the minute I get out. Looks
as though you could use some more of the hydrogen
peroxide.'

'Sure. Give us some more of that, please. And we'll
take a few more packs of the chromic 2–0 catgut
sutures, and some of the ligatures as well, Bonnie
Mae.' Craig spoke directly to Bonnie Mae, with that
warm, caressing note in his voice that Meg knew so
well. In spite of herself, she felt a certain chagrin, and
a reluctant nostalgia for the time when she had so
often been the focus of that warmth. She busied herself
writing the patient's levels on the anaesthetic sheet,
pretending a nonchalance that she did not feel, while
the other nurse went about replenishing supplies.
When Meg was alone with the two doctors, Craig did
not so much as look at her.

Bonnie Mae glided back into the room noiselessly
after an absence of fifteen minutes. 'Go have some
tea, Meg,' she whispered. 'It's in the office. Take about
twenty minutes. . .I'll watch the patient. This is likely
to go on for some time.'

'Thanks, I could use some tea.'

Outside the operating-room, Meg removed her face
mask, then the cotton cap that enclosed her hair and
made her scalp itch. With relief she ran her fingers

through her hair, then splashed cool water on her face
at the scrub sinks, before looking around her again
curiously. The medical station was relatively small, yet
compact and very well designed, the various buildings
separated by enclosed walkways so that the staff
did not have to go outside. In-patients were kept
to a minimum because there were not enough staff
to take care of them, so she had been told. People
like John Oldman would be shipped out, by air,
for long-term treatment when the immediate crisis
was over.

In the small staff office she poured herself tea. Sitting
in a chair, her feet propped up on another, she sipped
the hot tea with pleasure and helped herself to biscuits
from a tin. It was good to be out of both the hothouse
atmosphere of Gresham and the isolation of the
Manitoba nursing station, if she could manage to keep
an emotional distance from Craig. At least here she
had colleagues.

At University Hospital she had thought she was
secure in her job, even though there had been rum-
blings along the internal grapevine that the hospital,
along with most others, was in serious financial diffi-
culties. Rumours had been rife, adding daily to the
general feelings of insecurity. Staff at all levels were
being 'let go'—how she hated that term! Then it had
happened to her, on the last hired, first fired basis,
among other things.

Some of the other nurses with whom she had worked
had begun to wonder out loud whether the enigmatic
Dr Craig Russell, who so often asked for her to scrub
for him, was developing a 'thing' for her, and vice
versa. . .the very private Dr Russell who never dated
any of the nurses and who, it was rumoured, had dis-
creet affairs with some of the female doctors who came
within his orbit, affairs that never lasted more than a

few weeks. . . Dr Russell who had a small son but had not actually ever been married.

At first, for quite some time, there had been an air of abstraction about his interest in her—intense yet somehow reluctant. Her emotional antennae had informed her that he was somehow not available. . . not yet. She had tried not to listen to gossip, yet some of it had been unavoidable.

The clunking sound that the double doors to the OR in the medical station made when they were opened, then the heavy footsteps that came swiftly along the narrow passage towards her, gave her only a few seconds to compose her features into something approaching nonchalance before the object of her thoughts came into the office to join her. He had also removed his cotton cap, to reveal hair that curled damply around his lean, attractive face.

'Don't get up,' he said in a cool, clipped tone.

'I wasn't going to,' she said. 'Am I in your way?'

'You are. . .but I like seeing your legs stretched out like that, especially as I haven't seen them for a very long time.' To her heightened perception, the innuendo in his voice told her that she was indeed only the sex object that she had latterly perceived herself to be with him.

'That's surprising.' Meg compressed her lips briefly, pretending that his closeness did not affect her. 'There's more to me than legs,' she said.

'I know,' he said, while he poured himself a mug of tea. The light words lacked the bantering tone that had prevailed between them in their old life, yet they made her feel hot all over. There was a controlled tension in him. 'Tell me again why you left Gresham. . .preferably in words of one syllable, as briefly as possible, since we don't have much time. I had asked you to wait for me. Remember?'

Meg swung her legs to the ground and stood up. A slow flush spread over her cheeks as she faced him. 'As I said, I was fired,' she announced, 'or as good as. I had heard that the cosmetic surgery service at the hospital was to be cancelled to make way for more reconstructive plastic surgery; that was after you had repeatedly asked the head nurse if I could always be your scrub nurse for cosmetic surgery. You should know that any expression of preference like that creates resentment eventually, especially then. I became a victim of internal politics, you might say.'

'Aren't you exaggerating? The cosmetic surgery was to be moved to a clinic, not cancelled,' he said coldly.

'I happened to work at the hospital, not at a clinic,' she said. 'I suddenly found myself underemployed while you were away, by deliberate manipulations, I suspect. Then I was out. . .permanently. And don't tell me I'm paranoid. . . Everyone was very scared for their job. If you were immune to it, you were very lucky.'

'You're saying that I somehow engineered all this so that you would be thrown out? That's absurd,' he said curtly.

'I'm saying that you should have been sensitive enough to know what was likely to happen there if you showed what could be construed as favouritism. After all, you were an old hand; I was new and pretty green. How green I'm only just realising. The atmosphere was awful. . .'

How could she make him understand what it had been like for her, without sounding rabidly paranoid? She knew she hadn't imagined it. . . It had all been horribly real. . .the envy, the back-stabbing, the awareness of professional position. Then, later, there had been the sexual envy. . . At the moment there was no way that she could bring herself to tell him

about that, if ever. About how she had found out that
he had only been playing with her, with her emotions,
that she was someone who could be picked up and
discarded on a whim, because he already had someone
else as a probable replacement for the mother of his
son. She hadn't known what to believe.

'I'm unconvinced. You were. . .are. . .an excep-
tionally good OR nurse. You shouldn't have left
Gresham in such a hurry. I understand you didn't even
work the two weeks notice that you were entitled
to. . .you went after one week,' he said.

'I. . .just wanted to get out. I couldn't afford my
apartment any longer either, to live in the middle of
an expensive city,' she said. It was impossible to
explain now that she had wanted to get away from
the head nurse, Joyce Travers, with whom a working
relationship had become difficult, largely because
of him.

It had been hinted at by one of the other nurses,
too, that Craig had wanted to get her out of the hospital
so that he could have a full-blown affair with her, then
to persuade her to come to work for him privately. At
the time she had thought it crazy. 'Don't tell me you
gave a damn about what happened to me,' she said.
'A nurse, just one of the crowd? I don't suppose you
came up here to find me.' The bitterness that she felt
fuelled the sarcasm in her voice, even though she knew
at the back of her mind that she was perhaps making
him responsible for more than he had had the power
to control.

'Don't impute motives to me, or lack of them,' he
said in a tight voice that vibrated with anger. 'Why do
women get bitchy when they have sex with a man,
then find that there's no sort of pay-off? As though
they don't enjoy it themselves for what it is, pure and
simple?'

'That's. . .that's a really rotten thing to say. . .' she whispered, horrified.

'Is it? Let's get one thing really clear. I enjoyed having sex with you, you're a very attractive woman, but now I wouldn't touch you with the proverbial barge pole.' He leaned forward and gripped her upper arms so that she was forced to hold his gaze with her own. 'Just so that you know not to do the shrinking maiden bit when we're sharing accommodation. I can get what I need elsewhere.'

'How dare you?' she said, her pride stung beyond endurance. 'You arrogant, assuming——'

'Yes, I dare! And what makes you think I could control those decisions you're on about? If people get hurt in the squeeze, that's the name of the game.' He was so close to her now, glaring down at her tautly, that her nostrils were filled with the familiar, barely perceptible scent of the cologne that he wore, mingled with the masculine scent of his skin. 'If you can't stand the heat, don't play with fire.'

'What are you talking about?'

'I think you know, on both counts.'

'Let me tell you one other reason why I got out of Gresham so quickly.' She got the words out with difficulty, through lips that felt stiff with suppressed emotion. 'Various people warned me about you. . .' She had not really meant to admit that; normally she would give a person the benefit of the doubt until she was given cause to think otherwise. Now she wanted to hurt him as he had hurt her.

They were both breathing rapidly. 'Oh, yeah? Who?'

'Some of the nurses.'

'That figures! Spare me the details,' he said bitterly.

There was a short, uncomfortable silence.

'As a matter of curiosity only, where did you go after you left Gresham?' he demanded harshly.

'I. . . To Northern Manitoba. . .' Meg found herself stammering. 'To a—a place called Jasper Creek. It has a nursing station, the only one for miles around.' She looked pointedly at the clock. 'I. . .I have to go back to the OR; I've been out for nearly twenty minutes.'

Craig Russell gripped her arms more firmly as she tried to leave, towering over her. 'Listen, I don't want you bearing any grudges against me. This is not the sort of place where grudges are wise. It's one hundred per cent co-operation here. From now on, it's strictly business. Outside of work I don't give a damn what you do, so long as it has nothing to do with me. Agreed, Miss Langham?'

'Yes, that's quite all right with me. . .Dr Russell.'

'Good! Remember that! We'll get through these weeks somehow.' He let go of her then, giving her a little push of dismissal as he moved away, turning from her. 'Tell them I'll be in there in about ten minutes.'

Knowing that his remark had given her an excuse to leave quickly, she hurried on numbed legs back to the area of the scrub sinks, feeling as battered as though she had been in a physical fight, her tears barely under control. Automatically she put on a clean OR cap, carefully pulling it down over her ears, pushing up every wisp of hair into it. Her heart was pounding fearfully as she tried to calm herself by going through the familiar routine of tying her mask on, slowly, deliberately. Even in her anguish she wondered why he was being unnecessarily cruel. Was he, perhaps, protesting too much? Anyway, it was all going to be far worse than she had thought.

Craig Russell was not a man one could leave with equanimity; if she had missed anyone in Jasper Creek, it had been him. Certainly she had thought about him a lot. . .and not always with hostility; in fact she had longed for him. Now she could see that the reunion was to have its own terrors.

Bonnie Mae appeared to notice nothing amiss when Meg came back to the operating-room. The mask hid the spots of colour on her cheeks.

'Dr Russell said he'd be back in about ten minutes,' she announced, to no one in particular.

'OK,' Bonnie Mae answered. 'You'll get your tea then, Alanna.'

Meg took over again at the anaesthetic machine, her eyes going to the digits on the monitors, her mind numbed by the bitter verbal exchange she had just endured. Work was going to be her balm. This weekend, which was meant to be her time of rest and orientation, was obviously going to continue to be very busy. John Oldman would need constant care, twenty-four hours a day, until he was recovered enough to be flown out of Chalmers Bay to the city many miles to the south. She would take her turn with his post-operative care.

Skip, the OR technician, who was off duty for the weekend, would be there on Monday, so Bonnie Mae had told her. He would be at the medical station for the next two weeks, then was due to take off for a refresher course down south. Alanna Hargrove would be flying out in a day or two, as soon as a new doctor arrived to take her place, sponsored by the Northern Medical Development Corps.

Well, the nursing station in Manitoba had prepared her well for all this, Meg thought, with a certain grim satisfaction; she could endure, even if she had no private life to speak of. While there, she had taken copious notes of all the patients and their problems that she had had to deal with on her own. This was what she wanted. . .to be challenged, to be in the forefront of the action. That was one of the reasons why she had always loved working in the operating theatres.

Craig came back into the room, his arms dripping water from the scrub sink. Meg was aware of his presence, like an electric current in the room, an invisible cord between them, even now, in their animosity. She avoided looking at him.

John Oldman was in a lot of pain when the anaesthetic wore off. His limbs were heavy with bandages that were stained here and there with pinkish blood; his protruding hands and feet were swollen and bluish. The surgeons had done their best to ensure that they had repaired enough of the mangled arteries and veins so that he would have a sufficient blood supply to his limbs. There was always the possibility of necrosis— dying tissue—and gangrene.

They were in the small recovery-room beside the OR. Meg, who had volunteered to take a turn looking after him, in spite of her fatigue, while Bonnie Mae slept, injected a pain-killing drug by slow increments into the intravenous tubing that dripped clear fluid into a vein in John Oldman's neck.

'This will take away the pain, Mr Oldman,' she said, bending close to him so that he could hear her. Then she adjusted the naso-gastric tube which passed through one of his nostrils down to his stomach, and which enabled her to give him oral fluids and to aspirate the stomach contents if necessary.

He muttered a word of thanks when she moistened his dry lips with cool water and washed his face. 'My wife. . .?' he whispered.

'The RCMP is trying to contact your wife. . .and the rest of your family,' she assured him. 'Perhaps they've already done it by now. Try not to worry. They'll get flown up here to see you as soon as possible.' Someone, Meg knew from past experience, would volunteer to cover the cost of such a mercy flight. Perhaps a charter company would do it.

A youngish man, in his thirties, John Oldman looked the epitome of his proud race, with thin features, black eyes and rich blue-black hair that fell to his shoulders. He and his people knew how to live off the land in a harsh terrain, how to hunt, trap, fish, how to survive the bitter winters, how to build shelters and boats from natural resources. As Meg watched over him until his eyes closed again and his frown of pain, silently endured, disappeared, she felt a renewed respect for him and his people. Many of her patients in Jasper Creek had been from Indian tribes too, so she well understood their resilience and courage.

She mixed more antibiotics for injection into one of the plastic bags of intravenous fluid, so that the drug would flow continuously into his damaged body, where the risk of severe infection was very great. It was possible also that the bear had had rabies, so they were taking steps to cover that as well. When that was done, she brought all her charts up to date, checking the monitors that automatically recorded the vital signs.

The wall clock showed her that they were well into the early hours of the morning when Craig walked in quietly as she bent over the charts, making notes. 'Everything OK?' he said, his voice neutral. There was a stubble of dark hair on his face and he looked tired.

'Yes, I think so. He's fairly stable, although his blood-pressure's a bit on the low side at times, and I'm worried about his feet; they're rather blue.' How absurd it felt that they should be so formal when she had been pining for him for eight months, when they had exchanged fiery insults so recently.

'Mmm. . . Keep him warm, as I see you are doing.' He lifted the blankets to inspect John Oldman's feet.

'We might need some extra warmth with hot-water bottles and maybe a heat lamp.'

'Yes, I'll organise it. Here's the chart.' Meg handed it to him. 'He's having the continuous antibiotics and I've just given him more Demerol for the pain.'

'Good. Tell Bonnie Mae, when she comes, to keep that going all night. I see you've got the adrenalin and other stuff handy in case his blood-pressure drops any more, although I don't want to risk reducing the peripheral circulation. Tell Bonnie Mae to call Dr Hargrove right away if there's any change; she's officially on call from now on.'

'Yes, I will.'

'Give him oxygen and keep the IV fluids going. I'll take some blood for a haemoglobin before I go. If it's down, I want to put up another IV line.'

They moved out of earshot of the patient. 'Is he going to be all right?' Meg whispered, unable to suppress a fearful premonition.

'It's touch-and-go,' Craig said soberly, echoing her thoughts. 'If we can get him through the night and tomorrow morning, he should be OK. How much blood have we got left that's cross-matched?'

'Three units,' she said. 'There's some plasma, too.' Then she took out some blood-collection tubes, syringes and hypodermic needles from a drawer in the recovery-room office area. 'Here's the stuff for the haemoglobin.'

He put the things in the pocket of his lab coat.

'I. . .I just don't want him to die,' she whispered, wanting a few words of reassurance from him. Indeed, she was stricken, felt tears gathering in her eyes. No doubt her weakness was partly due to her need for rest after her journey to Chalmers Bay.

'We're going to do our very best to make sure that he's OK. . .aren't we?' he countered brusquely. 'This isn't some third-rate team we've got here. If he makes it we'll get him out as soon as he's OK to make the journey to Edmonton.'

Meg nodded. John Oldman's face, drawn with pain, pale from loss of blood, was firmly fixed in her mind's eye so that she knew she would never forget it.

When Craig had gone, after he had put in a second IV line and started to run in more blood, it felt unreal to her that they were both working in this small place, in the back of beyond, when they had in the past been in a far different context. Tonight she would sleep in the staff annexe, knowing that he was not very far away, could be there if necessary in about five minutes. That thought was somehow reassuring, in spite of everything.

With her attention once again fully on John Oldman, the minutes ticked by quickly until Bonnie Mae appeared to relieve her, having managed to snatch a few hours' sleep.

'How's it going, Meg?' she said, coming into the room with her curious rolling walk, carrying a bag of supplies, like coffee in a flask, to see her through what was left of the night. Already she had confided to Meg that she ate too much through the long weeks of winter in Chalmers Bay, which was why she was so fat, that she was engaged to be married to one Chuck Melvin, a freight pilot with a charter company in the Arctic, who frequently came to Chalmers Bay to spend time with her. While new people came and went, Bonnie Mae remained constant.

'Hello, Bonnie,' Meg smiled. 'Glad to see you.'

When she had given the report, she lingered for a while to talk to Bonnie Mae while John Oldman slept peacefully under the influence of the narcotic.

'Do you get fed up with new people coming here all the time, Bonnie?' Meg asked curiously, watching her colleague organise herself efficiently.

'Sometimes. . .but other times no. It gives me a bit of variety, other points of view. . .and I learn new things from other people. Some I could do without,' she chuckled, 'but just lately the NMDC has been getting some really good people, good doctors, to come up here—makes a change, I can tell you—and trying to persuade them to come back for a number of weeks or months each year, to keep up a certain continuity. This is the second time that Alanna's been here, and the guy she married, Owen Bentall, he's been here several times. . .a great guy! They'll both be back.'

'It sounds a great idea,' Meg agreed, daring to speculate on whether Craig Russell would be back, or whether she would herself.

As though following her line of thought, Bonnie Mae commented, 'Craig's been to the Yukon several times, so I hear. Maybe he'll transfer his loyalties to the Northwest Territories, eh? If we treat him right?' She looked at Meg in what seemed to be a meaningful way. 'And what about you?'

Meg had not yet told her that she was well-acquainted with Craig. This did not seem to be the right time to tell her, since it would inevitably spark a discussion. 'Maybe,' she said non-committally. 'We'll see how it goes. Well. . .' she suppressed a yawn '. . .I must get some sleep. Goodnight. Hope everything goes well.'

'Tomorrow, or I should say this morning,' Bonnie Mae said, 'I'll take you around Chalmers Bay on the medical station's skidoo; that's the best way to get around right now. I'll show you the general store, the pharmacy, and we even have a small museum, mainly about the whaling days up here. A bit later on, when things start to warm up in earnest, we get the ice-breaking ships coming through the Gulf to open up a channel for us. The crews all come into Chalmers. I'll show you the docks. How about nine-thirty, after breakfast?'

'I'd love that, but won't you be tired?'

'No. . .I'll have the rest of the day to sleep. Alanna's going to spend the morning with Mr Oldman, then we have Nuna—an Inuit lady who comes in to help out. She's a nursing aide, really great; she'll deal with anything else while we deal with Mr Oldman. We can always get Skip to come in if we have to, although I don't like doing that because he works damn hard during the week.'

'OK, nine-thirty, then, Bonnie. I'm looking forward to it.'

'At Easter weekend there's going to be a carnival in Chalmers, with dog-sled races and all. You'll like that. Easter's a big thing up here; it's the end of winter. . .even though it don't seem like it,' she added ruefully. 'The Inuit call this time Opinraksak, early spring. Get Craig to take you to the carnival.'

'He's already got a. . .friend; I expect he'll take her. . .and his son,' she said, not pretending, before Bonnie Mae's perceptive eyes, that she would not like to go to a winter carnival with Dr Russell, in spite of everything.

'Aw, don't worry about her. She's going around with one of the RCMP guys, Greg Farley.'

'Oh. . .' Meg hid her surprise well as she turned to leave, calling out a soft 'goodnight'. Now what could that mean?

The night was clear and dark when she let herself into the annexe from the covered way, then she opened the other outer double doors that went directly outside. Standing on the top step, swathed in her parka, she breathed in the cold, dry night air for a few moments, felt the wind touch her face like cool fingers. A few

winking lights were dotted here and there over the flat
expanse of the village set in snow; they made reflected
funnels of pale yellow, cold light on the sea of white.
In the distance she could see the lighted outline of the
small control tower of the airstrip.

She was a captive in this place, with no roads out,
only the temporary ice roads that were formed across
the string of lakes that went south, starting some miles
over the tundra from Chalmers Bay. They would
become unsafe with the coming of spring, when the
ice, maybe thirty-six inches thick, would begin to thin
out and crack and no longer support vehicles. She
shivered with a strange longing.

What she had said to Alanna Hargrove about being
tough was not strictly true. It was only true on the
surface. She had had to be tough from an early age
in order to make a life for herself. Like the ice roads,
she could thin out and crack in this place, being in
proximity to the man with whom she had a love-hate
relationship. Inside, she was soft, vulnerable . . .
because she didn't think he could ever be for her. . .

Looking east, up above the covered way to the medical station, she saw with a sudden thrill the dancing
northern lights in the dark sky. Shimmering bands of
mysterious light moved down towards the horizon,
gauzy patterns of green and white darted here and
there like fairy-wings.

Silence reigned over the outdoors, only now and
then disturbed by the strange moaning of the wind,
like an animal that never slept. Meg went inside.

CHAPTER THREE

'THAT'S the Royal Canadian Mounted Police headquarters—the RCMP,' Bonnie Mae yelled over her shoulder, gesturing with an arm, as they sped through Chalmers Bay on the skidoo the next morning, going considerably faster than Meg had travelled in the pick-up truck two days before.

'Yes. . .' Meg yelled back. 'If you don't watch out they'll arrest you for speeding, at the rate you're going!'

'They know me,' Bonnie Mae shouted jubilantly. 'I always go fast! They'll think it's a medical emergency! Whee!' She revved the engine still more and the elegant machine, like a large sled on skis, with a blunt, shiny black metal nose, rose up over a small mound of frozen snow in their path and came down the other side with a stomach-lurching swoop, causing Meg to let out an involuntary scream.

'You're a homicidal maniac, Bonnie Mae! Are you trying to make work or something?' she shouted.

'Relax and enjoy it! At least you won't get pregnant on this thing! That's the Anglican church over there.' She gestured in another direction, so that Meg fought to turn her head the right way to see the church, battling against the violent slip-stream of wind that was ever present on the open skidoo. 'There's the church hall next to it; we have a lot of functions there—dances and so on.'

Meg hung on for dear life as Bonnie Mae turned the machine down an alley beside the church, out the other side into a lane. . .or what would be a lane when the snow melted.

'There's the general store and post office, there's the museum over there, and the craft shop.' Bonnie Mae kept up a running commentary. 'Hang on! We'll take a quick look at the docks. . .not much to see yet. . .then I want to call in on a patient. OK?'

The docks looked forlorn, deserted. Huge, convulsed waves and outcrops of ice were spread over Coronation Gulf where the turbulent water had frozen in the shapes that the first intense freezing weather had found it in at the beginning of winter, not flat and neat as one always thought of ice, like a skating rink. Soon it would begin to break up.

They headed back to the centre of the village, where Bonnie Mae brought the machine to a sweeping halt in front of a small, squat house made of metal-clad wood which looked well-insulated against the outdoors. Smoke rose above the roof from a thin metal chimney stack. Bonnie Mae heaved her snow-suited bulk off the skidoo, inviting Meg to do the same.

'This is the home of Charlie Patychuk, one of our patients. I usually come to see him several times a week and I want you to meet him. He's old and got a weak chest, old TB case. There's quite a bit of TB up here, though not as bad as it used to be in the bad old days of the Fifties, of course, before they had any drugs. His daughter will make us tea, if we smile at her nicely.'

The door was opened before they had even got up the steps of the small front porch. A short, thin woman with a smiling face held the door open for them while they hurried in out of the cold, their boots squeaking in the frozen snow. 'Hi!' she greeted them. 'Nice to see you. *Teagukpin?*'

'*Ii, matna,*' Bonnie Mae replied. 'This is another nurse. . .Meg. And, Meg, she wants to know if we would like tea, so I said yes. OK?'

'OK,' Meg agreed, shaking hands with the Inuk woman.

In the main living-room sat an old man, and when they entered it a boy joined them from another room, a boy who looked to be about fourteen, as far as Meg could judge. 'Hi, Bonnie Mae.' The boy spoke first, his smile a mixture of shyness and delight at seeing visitors whom he obviously welcomed. 'It's nice to see you.'

'Well, Tommy, and how are you? My! I think you've grown a couple of inches since I last saw you. . .all of two weeks ago! Eh?'

'Yeah. . .I do seem to be growing,' the boy agreed. 'It's about time.'

'Meg, this is Tommy Patychuk, and this is his grandfather, Charlie Patychuk.' As Meg shook hands with both of them she noticed that the boy's hands were dreadfully scarred along the backs, the skin a livid pink. Above the collar of his shirt and sweater the skin of his neck was similarly scarred.

Seeing the line of her gaze, Bonnie Mae explained, 'Tommy was in a very bad fire last year. . .got awfully burned. . .spent a lot of time down south, getting himself fixed up.' She spoke very gently, yet matter-of-factly, as though she knew that the boy would not wish to be the object of anything that smacked of pity. At least his face, thin and handsome, had been spared.

The old man sat in a comfortable chair, his creased face telling a story of a lifetime of harsh living in the north. His hands, which he held quietly in front of him, were deformed and calloused, the fingernails blackened and broken. In this community he would have a respected social position as an elder.

'Hello, Mr Patychuk,' Bonnie Mae addressed him. 'You OK today?'

'*Ii*,' he nodded, a little nonplussed, Meg could tell, by being confronted with someone he had never seen before.

The tea, made by throwing tea leaves directly into a kettle of boiling water, was strong and good, sweetened with condensed milk from a tin. As they drank it, Bonnie Mae conversed with the family about community events and affairs, lapsing easily into the local language, Inuktitut, when she thought it necessary, while Meg listened. Her colleague did her the courtesy of translating every now and then, while Tommy chipped in to explain a few things as well.

'We all share here, and those who have food give to others who have not,' he said simply, letting her know that he was aware that it was not the same down south. 'Others' worries are our worries, their joys are our joys.'

They both drank a second cup of tea. They would not stay long, this being a Sunday, because the family would soon be getting ready to go to church.

Back at the medical station, with the skidoo safely parked in its special garage, Bonnie Mae departed to sleep and Meg let herself into the annexe. It would be a relief to get out of the thick parka and snow-pants that made walking cumbersome, not to mention the wide, padded boots.

'Hello, Meg.' Alanna's voice greeted her before she had even closed the inner door. 'Are you frozen solid?'

'Not quite,' she said through lips stiff with cold, her voice muffled behind the scarf that had protected the lower half of her face. To her discomfiture, she saw that Craig was sitting in their living area, looking very much at home in casual clothes, so that she felt suddenly shy and ill at ease, as though she was an intruder, somehow in an anomalous position, and her previous buoyant spirits deserted her. She busied herself removing her boots and the layers of outer clothing.

'We're having a sort of early lunch. . .brunch, really. You look as though you could do with some hot soup.'

'Um. . .yes, please. Hope I'm not interrupting a medical conference,' Meg answered, avoiding a direct glance at Craig.

'Actually, we were having a conference of sorts,' Craig drawled, stretching his arms indolently above his head. 'About John Oldman. A good thing you're here; you might as well be in on it.'

'Is he still all right?' she asked, hanging her outer clothing on a peg near the door, so that she could continue to avoid looking at him. He was certainly putting on an act for Alanna's sake. 'Bonnie Mae told me he had survived the night. That's good news.'

'Yes. The circulation to his limbs is a little better too, but not as good as we would like it to be,' Craig said, addressing her directly, 'and our dilemma is that we would like to ship him out to a big centre where they have the equipment to oxygenate his tissues, but he might not make the journey the way he is now. We might get as far as Yellowknife. . .' His voice trailed off thoughtfully.

'Yes, I see. . .' Meg agreed. 'It is a problem. Who would go with him on the aircraft?'

'Probably Bonnie Mae,' Alanna said. 'Or I could take him when I go, if he's in a condition to be moved. My replacement, Dr Dan McCormick, will be coming up as soon as he can get a direct flight, and the weather permits.'

'I see,' she said. Being a novice in this place, Meg decided to keep in the background for now. One thing about Craig Russell that was in his favour was that he

was not patronising. If only she could trust him in the
personal sphere as implicitly as she trusted him in the
medical sphere.

'Help yourself to soup, Meg. It's on the stove,'
Alanna invited.

'Thanks.'

Meg escaped to the kitchen. As she poured herself
soup she contemplated how soon she could escape
to the inner sanctum of her room without seeming
stand-offish. It had not occurred to her that the
doctors would use this sitting-room for medical con-
ferences, which would cut down considerably on her
privacy.

'Can you do the evening shift again today, Meg?'
Alanna came into the tiny kitchen to join her. 'That
will give you time to sleep now, if you want to. I'm
sorry it's worked out this way. . .not much time for
an orientation so far, but that's the way it is up here,
all so unpredictable. We get a lot of accidents. . .some
from the mines around here too, although they have
their own paramedics in the first instance, the search
and rescue teams, et cetera.'

'Don't worry about me,' Meg said yet again. 'I
got used to being on call twenty-four hours a day,
every day in Jasper Creek. One gets used to being
constantly alert.'

'Yes, I know. None the less, we'll try to make it up
to you. In the meantime, since I was up twice during
the night, I'm going to get a bit of sleep soon, before
the fray again tonight. Craig has kindly agreed to hang
about here for a while.'

Trying to hide the look of alarm that Meg knew was
in her eyes, she bent her head and carried her soup
through to the dining-table and sat with her back to
Craig. As soon as she was finished she would leave
them to it and go over to see John Oldman, to see for

herself how he was doing. A restlessness had engulfed her once more.

A natural opportunity came for her to make a temporary departure when the cook from the medical station's kitchen came in to replenish the ice-box and remove some of the empty dishes. He let himself in from the covered way just as Meg was finishing her second bowl of soup.

'Meg, this is Joe Fletcher,' Alanna introduced them. 'He cooks for us when we need him, and for the RCMP too, plus a few other outfits up here.'

Joe was of medium height, rangy and thin, with sunken cheeks and a mobile, humorous face.

'Howdy!' he said, shaking Meg's hand vigorously. 'So here's another one fool enough to spend time up here, eh?' His slow, twangy drawl indicated that he came from somewhere in the United States. 'Now why would anybody want to be up here when they could be someplace else more agreeable. . .like Wyoming, for instance, bringing in the steers, riding over the plains? I ask myself that question every day. . .and you know what I answer myself?' He did not wait for anyone else to offer an answer. 'It's the sheer cussedness of human nature, that's what it is! We won't let ourselves be beat, even if it means freezing to death trying to prove something. Been here seven years. I'm what they call a sour dough. . .sour about being here, but with not enough dough to get out!'

When he let out a shout of laughter, the others joined in. Meg suspected that he said this to every newcomer, as a sort of introductory performance, and she warmed to his effort. 'Maybe you stay because you're appreciated,' she suggested. 'You make great soup.'

'Why, that's mighty nice of you to say so, ma'am,' he said, putting on the act of the old bumpkin cowboy.

'Any time you want me to cook summat for you, you just get on the old blower. I can do a lot more'n soup.'

'Thank you,' Meg said, smiling. 'I look forward to your efforts.'

Out of the corner of her eye she observed Craig looking at her sardonically. When Joe went to replenish their ice-box, she took the opportunity to go to her room to collect a lightweight jacket and let herself out to the covered way.

The clinic area was quiet, deserted. Since the medical station lacked a separate intensive care unit, any very seriously ill patients who required constant monitoring were kept in the recovery-room until they were well enough to be moved to one of the few holding beds that they had in a tiny ward area. John Oldman was still in the recovery-room, but would have to be moved out tomorrow to make way for the patients on the operating list who were coming in for day surgery. Bonnie Mae had told her that they usually had an operating list on Mondays, Wednesdays and Fridays.

As soon as Meg saw John Oldman, some of her anxiety about him lifted. A middle-aged Inuit woman was standing beside his stretcher spooning something into his mouth from a bowl. If he was able to eat, he must be feeling a lot better. As Meg approached, he moved his head to look at her, appearing alert, although still pale.

'Hello, I'm Meg Langham, the new nurse,' she said. 'You must be Nuna. I'm going to be relieving you this afternoon.'

'Hi! Yes, I'm Nuna. Pleased to meet you. He's improving.'

Nuna was short and squat, with a round, plump face that creased up when she smiled, making her look motherly. Her movements were deliberate, capable. 'The RCMP called to say they had managed to contact

Mr Oldman's wife,' Nuna informed her. 'They are of the Dene tribe, further south. Maybe she will come in today, if they can get a plane coming up. We are getting more blood coming up too, from the blood bank at Yellowknife. Maybe it will arrive later.'

'That's great news. Well, I'll see you later, Nuna.'

'Sure!'

Well, that was a relief, Meg conceded as she walked towards the outpatient section of the medical station, taking this opportunity to explore the clinic area while no one was there. Various clinics were held there every week, usually on Tuesdays and Thursdays.

As she was exploring, she heard an outer door open and close, first the squeak of the metal storm door, then the inner door, then the sound of footsteps. Going out into a narrow passage, she came face to face with a woman clad in outdoor gear, a fur-trimmed hood pulled close around her head.

'Oh. . .hello. You must be the new nurse. I just came in on the off-chance. . .looking for Bonnie Mae,' the woman addressed Meg, pushing back the hood to reveal an anxious face, quite young. 'I. . .I guess she's not here, eh?'

'No, I'm afraid not. She was working during the night, so she's sleeping. Could I help perhaps?'

'I was hoping I could see someone privately, without having to make an appointment for the clinic. You see, I don't want my family to know about it yet.' The woman, a white woman from down south, was obviously very worried about something. 'My name's Adele James. . .Bonnie Mae knows me well. . . My husband's an RCMP officer here in Chalmers; we're here on a two-year rotation. The point is. . .I've got a breast lump. I first noticed it about a week ago.'

'I see,' Meg said gently. 'Have you had lumps before?'

'No, never. So I'm really scared. . .absolutely terri-
fied, actually. You know, you read all these magazine
articles about breast cancer. . .' Her voice trembled
and trailed into silence.

'Well, there are two doctors here at the moment,
over in the staff annexe. I'm sure one of them would
see you now,' Meg offered. 'Would you like that? Or
would you prefer to see Bonnie Mae? I'm Meg
Langham, by the way.'

'Hello, Meg.' Adele James seemed distracted, obviously fighting to keep her fear under control now that
she had plucked up courage to come for help. 'Well,
I'll have to see a doctor eventually, won't I, so I might
as well see one now. . .if they don't mind that I haven't
got an appointment?'

'No, that's what we're all here for. Now, why don't
we go into one of these examination cubicles over here
and you can take off your top things and put on a
surgical gown, then I can take a quick look at the lump
before I go over to get one of the doctors? Do you
have medical records here? I can look them up while
you get changed.'

'OK. . . Thank you.' There was resigned relief in
the woman's voice now that the wheels were in motion,
so to speak. 'Yes, I do have records here.'

Meg found the woman's medical record folder in a
cupboard in the small office area of the outpatient
department. There had been no serious illness. Adele
James had two children, both born before she
had come to Chalmers Bay. Her trips to the clinic
had been mainly for routine check-ups, once for a
chest X-ray.

In the cubicle Meg helped Mrs James on to the
examination couch. 'You lie here and try to relax,' she
suggested. 'Show me where the lump is, then I'll go
over to the staff annexe to get one of the doctors.'

'OK. . . Thanks. It's right here—just on the under-side of my left breast.'

There was a definite lump. Meg could feel it easily, small but definitely palpable. 'Here's the blanket. Now, I won't be long. . .about ten minutes.' Taking the chart with her, she hurried back through the covered way, hoping to get there before Alanna had gone for her sleep.

The only person in the room was Craig, reading a newspaper, when she entered the sitting-room. 'Um. . .is Dr Hargrove still up?' she asked.

'No, she went to get some much needed sleep.' He stood up slowly, fixing her with his intent blue gaze. Judging by his appearance of exhaustion, he could do with some sleep too. 'I'm afraid you'll have to contend with me. Can I be of some assistance? I can see from the expression on your face that you're just bursting with news of some sort.'

Meg explained, handing him the woman's chart.

'Sure, I'll see her,' he agreed. 'Then I might head back to my place in town for a while. I can be contacted there if need be.'

'Yes. . .fine,' she said crisply.

'Glad to be rid of me?' he said perceptively, with a cynical amusement, looking at her closely as he pulled on his jacket.

'No, of course not.' She was determined to be strictly professional. Betraying colour crept into her cheeks.

'Liar,' he said softly. 'Come on, show me where this woman is.'

'Do you think it's cancer, Doctor?' Adele James queried, her voice high-pitched with apprehension, after Craig had examined her.

'It's hard to say from just palpating the lump. . .I don't think it is, but I would like to remove it as soon as possible, because it's always sensible to remove any breast lump, and to remove it quickly. We could fit you in on tomorrow's operating list if you could come in as a day-surgery patient. I would take out the entire lump, plus a little of the surrounding tissue, which is the routine procedure. I could do a needle-biopsy first, but that's a bit of a waste of time, especially since we don't have a pathologist up here.'

'Yes, I could arrange to come tomorrow,' their patient agreed. 'I haven't told my husband yet. . .'

'Good. The chances of it being cancer are not great. It's more likely a lump of fat, what we call a lipoma, or a fibrous lump. . .non-malignant.' Craig spoke gently yet not condescendingly. 'However, we can't rule out cancer until we've cut open the specimen and had a look at it. Both Dr Hargrove and I will take a look at it tomorrow, then we'll make some slides to put under the microscope. Whatever conclusion we come to, we'll send the specimen down to a pathologist in the city anyway. The report from there will take about three weeks to get back to us. We should be able to tell with a fair amount of accuracy, about eighty per cent, what we're dealing with tomorrow.'

'Thank you.'

'Is there any history of breast cancer in your family?'

'An aunt of mine, my mother's sister, had it. That's why I'm so scared.'

'Mmm. . .I'm glad you came to see us. That was the right thing to do. Can you get here by eight-thirty tomorrow? We'll do it under local anaesthetic, but don't have anything to eat or drink after midnight, just in case we decide to make it a general. OK?' Craig smiled at her, giving her shoulder a reassuring squeeze. 'Try to get a decent night's sleep.'

'I did breast-feed both my babies. . . That helps to guard against breast cancer, so I've heard. . . doesn't it?'

'Yes, it does seem to; we're not sure why. Are you otherwise in good health?' Craig asked kindly.

'Yes. . .as far as I know, I am.'

'I want to update your medical history, then take your blood-pressure, listen to your heart and lungs, then take a sample of your blood for a haemoglobin test to make sure that you're not anaemic, and to get your blood type.'

When the examination had been completed, Craig motioned Meg to join him in the staff office. 'Put her on the operating list, please. See where you can fit her in. . .the earlier the better, to put her out of her misery. And please tell Bonnie Mae when you see her later tonight.'

'Yes. . .'

'You have rather been thrown in at the deep end, haven't you?' Craig commiserated with her, surprisingly breaking through the barrier he had put up. 'I'm sure you can cope, though. How are you liking it here so far? I know it's early days.'

Meg looked at him sideways, not trusting this apparent effort he was making to be civil, after the crude words he had spoken to her only the day before. 'I think I'm going to find it interesting, challenging, rewarding. . .all those things,' she said truthfully. 'Fascinating too, of course. I saw the northern lights for the first time last night. They're amazing. . .and sort of fearful at the same time.' Meg found herself chattering quickly to mask the undeniable physical bond between them that still broke through the acute discomfort she now felt in his presence. Again she wondered about Rob's mother. . .

'Yes. Inuit lore says that the lights are the souls of

unborn children, dancing in the sky,' he said.

'Oh. . .' Meg breathed. 'Enchanting. . .'

'Anyway,' Craig said abruptly, his deep voice tinged now with an urgency to get away, his momentary aberration over, 'here's the operating list, on this notice-board. Now I'm going to take off. . .' He scribbled a telephone number on a piece of paper and gave it to her. 'This is where I can be reached, so don't hesitate if you want me. Maybe I'll look in again later. Gail will take a message if I'm not immediately available.'

'Um. . .Gail?' There was a cold tingling of recognition in her veins as she heard the name. So Joyce Travers had been right, it seemed. . .

'The woman I'm staying with.' His face was expressionless.

'All right. Well, goodbye. . . I'll just see Mrs James out.'

Meg walked out of the room, willing herself not to flush, taking the operating list with her, trying not to let him see that the name had meant something to her. That was the name that the head nurse in the OR at University Hospital had taunted her with, suggesting that Craig Russell was not for her. . . Gail, who had been, so Joyce had said, the best friend of Rob's mother. . .who had been there to offer solace to father and son. . .

'Thanks, Nurse. I'll see you tomorrow, then?' Adele James seemed calmer as she got ready to leave, now that something was definitely going to happen. 'I'd better make arrangements for someone to take care of the kids tomorrow.'

'Yes. Come back to this department in the first instance, the earlier the better. And don't forget, nothing to eat or drink after midnight. It will be very straightforward, and you won't have much pain after;

we'll give you some pain-killers to take home. Try not to worry too much.'

Meg saw her out of the door, and watched her walk away carefully on the frozen snow to a waiting pick-up truck.

She would worry, of course. . .who wouldn't? At least she would not have to wait for weeks, agonising over the possible verdict. Other communities that did not have a medical station were not so lucky. Work was very sobering, Meg reflected as she shut the door; what were her own petty personal problems compared with this? At least her life was not on the line.

As she was about to leave later, the telephone rang in the outpatient office. Tentatively she picked it up, wishing that Bonnie Mae were around to deal with things until she had the lie of the land a little more.

'Hi there! This is Greg Farley of the RCMP, ma'am,' a hearty voice informed Meg, when she had identified herself. 'I haven't yet had the pleasure of meeting you—something which will have to be rectified at the earliest opportunity, eh?'

'Yes, certainly.' Meg found herself smiling, then quickly sobered up, considering that she might soon have some sort of disaster on her hands.

'I'm calling, ma'am, to say that John Oldman's wife just flew into town and she's right here with us at Headquarters. She'll be staying with one of the RCMP families for as long as need be, just as soon as we can fix it up, until you guys up there decide what's going to happen to him. Now I'm calling to ask what would be a good time for the little lady to come up there and see her hubby, because I'm going to get her up there myself. Don't want to inconvenience you, like, by turning up at the wrong time.'

Suppressing a giggle, Meg considered the question. Greg Farley sounded like a character in a western movie. Perhaps he was likewise comparing her accent to something equally funny to him. 'Give me your telephone number, then I'll call you back in a few minutes, if I may.'

'Sure, sure. . . Maybe one of you guys could bring her back here again after the visit?'

'Yes, I'm sure we can.'

Nuna was busy trying to get Mr Oldman to cough up mucus from his lungs, to do some deep breathing and to change his position on the bed when Meg returned to the recovery-room, so she watched for a few minutes, admiring Nuna's efforts and technique. She had a gentle, encouraging air, yet one that brooked no refusal.

'Mr Oldman,' she finally interrupted, 'I've just had news that your wife has arrived. She can come just as soon as we tell the RCMP to bring her.'

Their patient sank back against the pillows, breathing heavily from the painful exertion. His eyes, tired and bloodshot, lit up briefly. 'Tell her. . .come now,' he said.

'OK with you, Nuna?'

'Sure.'

'I'll call back, then I'll get out the pick-up truck to take her back later.' Meg left to make the call. Then she would get dressed in her outdoor gear to try her hand with the truck. In Jasper Creek she had had the use of a pick-up truck; the one here was bigger and heavier, with enormous tyres. Maybe that would make it easier to drive.

The truck was kept in a shed near the back entrance of the medical station, where supplies could be unloaded when brought from the airstrip. Bright sunlight sparkled on the snow as Meg trudged round there. Although she desperately wanted to sleep, she forced herself to keep moving.

Having unplugged the engine heater that was always left on, she gingerly drove the unwieldy vehicle round to a parking space at the front of the medical station where another electrical outlet was situated so that the heater could be plugged in again to keep the engine from freezing up. Then she would be ready for the return journey of Mrs Oldman.

Another truck drove up to park beside her when she had completed the move and a RCMP officer got out, dressed in the regulation dark blue snow suit. 'Hi there!' He spoke first. 'You must be Meg. Hang on!' As she struggled to get down from the high cab, he came round to her side and lifted her down effortlessly. A big man, quite young, he looked the epitome of everyone's idea of a law-enforcement man. 'I'm Greg Farley.' He removed one of his heavy gauntlets to shake her hand.

'Hello, very pleased to meet you.' Meg covertly assessed him, this man who was also, with Craig, a friend to the as yet mysterious Gail. 'I've shaken more hands in the past two days than in the last two years, I think.'

'Sure! It's a friendly place here, ma'am. Or may I call you Meg?'

'Meg. . .please.'

'Right! And I'm Greg to you. I'll introduce you to Mrs Oldman.' He lowered his voice conspiratorially. 'Tell me. . .how's the hubby? Is he. . .y'know. . . OK?'

'Considering what happened to him, yes, he is OK. She won't be too shocked, I hope.'

'Great!' He led her over to his truck and the woman sitting there. John Oldman's wife was thin, tired-looking, a woman in her thirties. She had come a long way and looked it, so that Meg felt a flood of sympathy for her.

The woman was quiet and withdrawn as they entered the medical station, obviously very fearful of what she might find. Nuna had moved John to a semi-sitting position and had covered his limbs with sheets, Meg noted instantly as they entered the recovery-room. When he saw his wife he lifted his head and smiled, giving a long-drawn-out, 'Ahh. . .'

She went up to him quickly, put her cheek against his. Almost instantly she began to weep, a soft, sobbing cry, and as he leaned his head against hers tears seeped from his closed lids and ran down his cheeks. Nuna and Meg quietly left the room.

'I'm going to sleep, Nuna. Would you call me when she's ready to leave?' Meg whispered. 'I'll be over in my room.'

'Sure. She stay a long time.'

Tears formed in her own eyes as she walked through the covered way back to her room, and she wiped them away impatiently, because they were tears, she suspected, not just for John Oldman and his wife, but for herself too, for something that seemed impossible at that moment. Sleep was what she needed. She would sleep until Nuna called her.

The drive back to the police headquarters and return journey to the medical station went without mishap. Most of the day was already gone. An added chill was creeping into the air as Meg parked the truck, causing her to shiver violently. There would be time for a leisurely hot shower before she went on duty at three-thirty. Earlier, after her sleep, she had heard Alanna getting up and leaving the annexe, presumably to check up on Mr Oldman before Nuna left.

The shower felt wonderful, like thousands of hot, invigorating needles pricking her skin, bringing it back to tingling life. The bathroom had no bathtub, only a shower-stall enclosed by a door of frosted glass that had a wide gap at the top to let out the steam. She shampooed her hair, revelling in the feel of the streams of water running down her back from strands of hair. It was amazing how simple pleasures came to the fore, to be enjoyed anew, when nothing more sophisticated was available.

A knock came on her bedroom door. It would be Alanna. 'Come in,' she called over the top of the shower door. When she heard nothing, she shouted again, louder. Foam from the shampoo ran down her face and into her eyes, so she kept them closed, rubbing vigorously at her hair. When she opened her eyes again, having put her head under the shower stream to rinse off the soap, the person she saw standing in the bathroom was not Alanna.

'A very delectable sight, Meg Langham.' Craig Russell stood there in her tiny bathroom, his head and shoulders visible above the level of the dividing glass door, looking at her.

Water plastered her hair close to her scalp and over her face, so that she peered at him in shocked silence through a curtain of wet hair, each strand dripping water down into her mouth. Fumbling with the taps, she managed to get the water turned off.

'What the hell are you doing in here?' she said furiously, spitting a strand of hair out of her mouth, aware as she turned towards him that he could clearly see her entire outline through the lightly frosted glass. Indeed, his eyes moved, as though automatically, the length of her body and back again to her face. His own features were deadpan.

Not that it mattered really, she thought as she felt momentarily nonplussed, doing everything in slow motion; he was merely renewing an acquaintance with what had once, for a brief time, been familiar to him.

'I'm no prude, but I do prefer a little warning before a man comes into my bathroom, especially when he's uninvited.'

'You did yell "come in",' he countered, unsmiling. 'In fact, you said it twice. I was quite prepared to wait until you came out.'

'Well, I. . .I assumed it was Alanna. Did you have something to say to me?' she spluttered.

'I was looking for Alanna, actually. She wasn't over in the recovery-room,' he said laconically. From his casual stance, hands in pockets, as he leaned against the wall opposite her, she might have been a log of wood as far as he was concerned. Yet there was a tension in the air, which Meg knew was not coming just from her. 'I thought she might be in here with you; she's not in her room.'

'Well, she's not here either; you can look under the bed if you like. And I hope you don't think you can just waltz in here any time you want when you have a room here.' Meg stood squarely facing him. 'Or would you call that request "the shrinking maiden bit", or whatever it was you said, Dr Russell?'

There wasn't much point now, she considered, in doing an undignified three-point cover-up. She strove to maintain her initial indignation as she felt other, betraying emotions creeping over her, very conscious of the thin partition being all that there was between them. Her skin tingled with an awareness of his closeness.

Unexpectedly he leaned forward, reaching in over the door, to part the wet curtain of her hair so that he could see her face. 'Now you look less like a drowned mouse,' he murmured.

As she opened her mouth to give a stinging retort, he withdrew his arms, and as he did so the glass door came unlatched from its magnet clasp and swung slowly and gently outwards, while he moved back to accommodate it. As the door swung open it made a groaning noise, like a sound effect in a Gothic horror movie. The same thought must have occurred to both of them at the same time; Meg's eyes met his, a feeling of hysterical laughter bubbling up inside her, which she controlled only with an extreme effort, reading there a reluctant amusement. She could no more have made a grab for the door than she could have covered up her body.

For a few seconds they stood facing each other in silence, very still. 'Now that I have no modesty left,' she said as bitingly as she could, recovering, 'perhaps you'll hand me a towel from in there.' As he moved out, she stepped out of the shower-stall and positioned herself behind the bathroom door, making a mental note to shut and lock it in future.

'Here. . .' He handed her a towel that she had left on the bed. 'So you're working the evening shift?'

The question prevented her from shutting the door in his face, so she draped herself in the towel and stood in the doorway. 'Yes. Starting in about half an hour,' she said pointedly.

'I may come over again later to have a look at John. We've got to come to a definite decision soon about when to ship him out.' He took a few steps away from her, looking at her consideringly.

As she returned his look, she had to concede that he was very attractive in casual jeans and a sweater instead of the usual scrub suit. 'Yes. . .OK.'

'You don't have to hide in there; I'm not going to rape you,' he said, moving towards the door of her room.

'I didn't think you were. . .I know that's not your style,' she retorted.

'Oh, you know my style, do you? From gossip and

rumour, maybe? Or did you come to that conclusion
from personal experience alone?' he asked softly,
dangerously. Nonchalantly he put his hands in his
pockets again and surveyed her.

'Just. . .just go away, Craig,' she whispered vehe-
mently, a betraying catch in her voice.

Slowly he straightened up and took a deep breath,
as though he was about to say something. But then he
turned abruptly and went out through the half-open
door, closing it quietly behind him.

Meg held her breath, listening to his retreating
footsteps until she heard the slam of the outer
door, then she let it out in a rush and sank down on
the bed. The relief of his going was mingled with a
sharp, bitter disappointment. Had he made a move
towards her, had opened his arms to her, she knew
that she would have dropped the towel and run into
them. She was beginning to despise herself for such
longings.

In Gresham they had become lovers, for an all too
brief period, in an unexpected way, almost by accident,
so that afterwards she had wondered whether he ever
would have progressed to that stage with her if the
lights had not gone out at the party during one night
of that long, beautiful summer. . .if there had not been
that violent storm, that prolonged downpour of rain
that had caused a power failure and prevented her
from going home. By that time she had known him
for months.

It had been a farewell party at the hospital, given
by one of the surgeons who was leaving to take up a
post in Texas. All the operating-room staff had been
invited. It had turned out to be a fun party, informal
and noisy, with music and non-stop dancing. The
evening had been very hot and humid. Only towards
the end of the evening, very late, had Craig Russell

asked her to dance. In his arms she had felt tongue-tied, not sure how to behave outside the controlled code of behaviour that prevailed during working hours in the operating-room and which, in spite of the humour, the joking and tension-reducing wit that was common among the staff there, made interaction easy precisely because it was prescribed. Sexual tensions were kept firmly in hand.

Not that her silence had mattered much; any sustained conversation had not been possible. As they had continued to dance, through all the music changes, Craig had drawn her closer to him so that their bodies moved together, touching, so that she had felt she would faint with her longing for him. Tentatively, aware of watching eyes on them, she had reached up to put her arms around his neck, her five-foot-two-inch height increased by high heels.

Only when the lights had abruptly gone out and the band had stopped had they all been aware of flashes of lightning outside, followed by immense claps of thunder and the sound of a downpour. There had immediately been cat-calls from some of the doctors in the room, their inhibitions loosened by wine. Lewd jokes had been shouted back and forth in the general chaos.

'Let's get out of here.'

Craig bent down to speak the words in her ear. She followed him obediently, her hand in his, and he led her outside where they braved the rain to make a dash in the dark to his parked car, under cover near the hospital entrance. Before she was able to clamber into his silver-grey Buick she was soaked to the skin, her thin silk evening dress plastered to her body. As she slammed the car door, breathless and safe inside, suddenly deliriously happy, she saw one of the other nurses, Cynthia Parks, walking past, looking at her.

Cynthia, who was a friend of Joyce Travers. . . They had both been at the party. . .

Moments later, as though a signal had been given silently, they were in each other's arms and kissing with careless abandon, urgently, releasing the pent-up passion of the previous weeks since they had met. For a long time neither of them spoke as hungrily their mouths clung together and his hands easily found her soft breasts through the wet, revealing fabric of her dress. Excitingly, she was seeing a new dimension to him. . .Rob's father. . .surgeon and colleague. . .now lover. It was something that had existed only in fantasy. Incredulously she gave herself up to him.

'I want to make love to you, Meg,' he said at last, holding her away from him to look at her face, his own sensual with desire, yet serious, strained. 'Don't say no. Come back to my house with me. . .stay the night. . .please.'

Meg was sure that he knew about other men friends of hers, had seen her with them. Apparently he had no qualms about that. Neither, she found, did she. They were not serious. 'Yes. . .' she said.

Without touching her again, or uttering another word, he started the car and drove through the downpour to where he lived. Once inside he took her straight to his bedroom, gently took off her sopping dress and draped it over a chair. Then he took her in his arms and said to her, 'I've wanted you very, very much for a very long time.'

They spent the night and the next day together before he had to go away. Those hours had been a revelation to her. Her love for him had been confirmed irrevocably. That was how it had been. . .

CHAPTER FOUR

THE next day, Monday, Meg met Skip for the first time when the three nurses started work just as the sun was coming up. He was one of the local Inuit people, a young man who lived in the village with his wife and children. Going over to work so early, Meg was glad that she was not required to go out in the bitter cold, that she could remain in the warm cocoon of the medical station.

'It's a good thing John's wife came,' Bonnie Mae remarked as they hurried to commence work. 'She can sit with him, keep an eye on him to help us out.'

'Yeah. . .' Skip agreed. 'Come with me, Meg; I'll show you where we keep the trays of instruments, the sterile packs and other supplies. This is a hectic time because a lot of patients arrive at the same time. I got a lot of the things ready last Friday before I went home. First of all, we've got three diagnostic curettages; they won't take long, as you know. We send those specimens down to the city.' As he spoke, they hurried in to the OR and switched on the lights.

'There's an added breast biopsy, a lumpectomy, actually,' Meg said, 'which I put fourth on the list yesterday. If that isn't good, we can change it to later.'

'That's fine,' he said, flinging open the door of a large cupboard to reveal large pre-wrapped packs of sterile drapes and trays of instruments. 'OK. . .let's get this show on the road!'

For the next hour they worked quickly and to a purpose, with no wasted moves. They were to start

operating at half-past eight. They could hear skidoos
and the occasional truck arriving outside as their
patients converged on the medical station. Some would
come from the airstrip, having made the journey by
private plane from surrounding areas and mines. At
ten after eight, Meg left Skip to go to see what Bonnie
Mae was doing.

At eight-fifteen, both Alanna and Craig arrived,
attired in scrub suits, to make a start.

'Hello, Mrs James. How are you?' Meg greeted the
woman with the breast lump, who now lying on
a stretcher waiting her turn for her operation.

'Scared,' the woman replied feelingly. 'That's all I
can really say. A certain relief too. . .can't wait to get
it over.'

'I'll see you a bit later on in the operating-room.'

As it was, Meg was the one to scrub for the removal
of the breast lump, to assist Craig. Alanna had done
the three D and C's, the diagnostic curettages, in
record time.

'And how are you this morning, Miss Langham?'
Craig asked formally—no doubt for the benefit of his
other colleagues, Meg thought waspishly.

'Quite all right, thank you,' she replied blandly, turning her concentration on the instruments that she
had on the sterile table before her as Skip wheeled
Mrs James in through the double doors of the
operating-room.

Half an hour later the breast lump had been removed
in its entirety. There was a tension in the room as
Craig positioned the tissue in a metal dish, then cut it
neatly and carefully in half with a clean scalpel, with
Skip and Meg watching. Mrs James dozed peacefully
under the influence of a sedative.

'It looks like a fibro-adenoma to me. . .non-
malignant,' Craig said softly to his waiting audience.

'Skip, would you please ask Alanna to come in here to take a look at this as well?'

'Thank God for that,' Meg breathed.

'Yes. . .but we can't be one hundred per cent sure until we get a pathologist's report back from the city, so we have to be careful what we say to her, in case we have to rescind later,' Craig reminded her flatly.

Alanna put on a pair of sterile latex gloves when she came in, then made several more cuts in the specimen. 'I agree with you,' she said after a few minutes. 'It looks like a fibro-adenoma. I'm pretty sure. A good thing we've both done some pathology.'

'Yes. Good. Thanks.'

Adele James's relief took the form of tears when she was informed of the probable diagnosis later, after the sedative had worn off and she was in a state to comprehend what was being said to her. Meg was glad for her, and was able to spare some of her empathy for Craig who would have been the one to break the bad news to her had the diagnosis been otherwise. That was never an enviable task for anyone.

A long, hectic work day ended for Meg when Nuna came at about eleven o'clock in the evening to spend the night nursing John Oldman. It had been agreed earlier in the day that Mr Oldman would be flown out the next day, accompanied by his wife and Bonnie Mae, now that his condition had improved to the point where it was safe for him to make the taxing journey. The circulation in his limbs had improved somewhat and he was still on the intravenous antibiotics. With his departure they would no longer have any in-patients, which would mean that, barring emergencies, life at the medical station would return to reasonably regular hours, until the next time.

They had also heard that Dr Dan McCormick would be arriving soon, possibly the next day, and maybe on the aircraft that Bonnie Mae would be leaving on with Mr Oldman. Things seemed to be falling into place. There was so much going on at the medical station that Meg managed to keep her burgeoning apprehension at bay, most of the time, regarding the imminent change of residence for Craig when Alanna departed.

Adele James came back to the clinic the next day to have her dressing looked at, the outer layers replaced with more sterile packing and a supporting bandage.

'My husband was sure mad with me,' she confided to Meg, 'because I hadn't told him about this from the beginning, when I first found the lump. But he has enough on his plate, dealing with things up here, so I didn't want to add to that. No point in worrying him, I thought, until we really had something to be worried about.'

'Yes. . .I think you were right, really,' Meg answered, her gentle fingers making the final turn of the bandage, then securing the end with a metal clasp. 'It's difficult to know what to do in the early stage. You want to talk to someone, but you don't want to make too much of it. You're feeling better now, though?'

'Oh, yes! A thousand times better. Even though the doctor said his diagnosis was only eighty per cent accurate, I feel so relieved. I feel as though there's hope. You know, when you find a lump like that, you think you're under a death sentence. . . The knowledge of that colours your whole life and you can't get it off your mind for an instant.'

'Yes, prompt action is the best thing. I want you to come to see me again on Thursday to have a completely new dressing, a lighter one. Dr Russell will look at it then, and we'll take the stitches out some time next week.'

'That's great. Will there be much of a scar?'

'The incision will fade eventually to a thin white line, scarcely noticeable. There's going to be some bruising for a while, purple and yellow. That will go, of course.'

'If. . .if I did have cancer, what would be the next move?'

'Well, theories on treatments change every so often. At the present time, most women are given some radiotherapy, followed by chemotherapy, depending on the exact nature of the tumour and how far advanced it is. Sometimes they have drugs which block the uptake of oestrogen by the breast tissue, since hormones can make some types of tumour grow faster. . . It all depends on what the doctor thinks is right for the individual woman. But I honestly think you don't have to concern yourself about that now.'

'Thanks a lot, Nurse.' Adele James gathered up her outdoor clothing, ready to depart. 'See you Thursday, then.'

'Come sooner if you're worried about anything. Come any time.'

There was a clinic for all and sundry at the medical station, which had already drawn quite a lot of patients by mid-morning, some for changes of dressing and for a follow-up after operation. All routine operations, elective surgery, had been cancelled for the rest of the week because Bonnie Mae was leaving to go to Edmonton with John Oldman, not expecting to be back in Chalmers Bay until the Friday evening.

Skip came back from a short coffee-break. 'You go for your coffee now, Meg,' he offered. 'Bonnie Mae's in the office; she wants to say goodbye to you before she finally goes. They're leaving here in about ten minutes.'

'I'll go, then.' She stripped off her rubber gloves

and washed her hands. 'I've already said goodbye to
Mr Oldman and his wife. What do you think his
chances are, Skip. . .of recovering fully?'

'Well, unless he develops a bad infection that can't
be controlled, I think he should be OK. Basically, he's
fairly young and strong.'

'Yes. Let's hope he'll be all right. I don't suppose
we'll see him again up here.'

'It's not likely.'

As she hurried to the office, she found Bonnie Mae
just preparing to leave.

'Ah, I just wanted to wish you good luck, Meg,
before I take off,' Bonnie Mae said. 'Sorry you have
to be left so soon. Looks as though you're not going
to get the luxury of a formal orientation. Not to worry!
Hang in there, stay cool! Dan McCormick's an old
hand up here; he'll be with you soon. . . He's worth
his weight in gold and you'll really like him. Now
I'm off.'

Meg watched her stride off, a large, capable figure,
carrying her suitcase, then she thoughtfully poured herself a cup of coffee, catching sight of herself in a small
wall mirror as she did so, feeling a jolt of surprise at
how peaky and tired she looked. Her lips, devoid of
lipstick, were almost colourless; there were shadows
under her expressive green eyes that made her look
more than ever like a waif. It was to be expected really,
she supposed, since she had had very little sleep.

Dr Dan McCormick proved to be short and stocky,
with red hair and freckles. He arrived, escorted by
Craig, about an hour after Bonnie Mae and her patient
had departed for the airstrip, while Meg was rushing
about helping Skip with the outpatient clinic, trying to
find out where everything was kept, how the system
worked.

'This is Meg Langham,' Skip introduced her. 'She

may look young and inexperienced, but she's no dude, that's for sure!'

'Hello, Meg. Great to meet you,' Dr McCormick said, shaking her hand vigorously, while Craig stood back a little watching them. Dan had a slight Scottish lilt underlying his Canadian accent. He had eyelashes that looked almost white, making his eyes appear a little like daisies. The eyes themselves were a very pale grey-blue, inquisitive and humorous. 'I'm glad you're not a new recruit, still wet behind the ears.'

'She's definitely not that,' Craig said, an added insinuation in his tone that was lost on all but Meg, before the two doctors moved off so that Dr McCormick could reacquaint himself with the facilities.

'Where is he going to be living?' Meg enquired of Skip.

'He's got a girlfriend in the town. She's the manager at the bank here. . .doesn't want to marry him yet and go to live in Calgary, 'cos she thinks she won't get such a good and well-paid job down there. She's probably right.'

It was on the Saturday, after Bonnie Mae was back, that they had a small farewell get-together for Alanna. They all gathered in the sitting-room of the staff annexe, where the exuberance of Dan McCormick made up for any obvious strain in the social relationship between Craig and Meg that might have been apparent to the others. Joe Fletcher was there, having baked an impressive cake, thick with chocolate butter icing, for the occasion.

'You better not eat too much of that cake, Bonnie Mae,' Joe said in his laconic drawl, 'otherwise you won't get to see your toes when you walk!' He and Bonnie obviously had an ongoing teasing relationship.

'You keep quiet, Joe Fletcher,' Bonnie Mae

retorted, cutting herself a generous slice of the gooey mixture and dumping it ostentatiously on a plate, 'otherwise you gonna get a big fat lip to go with that big mouth of yourn.'

Joe tittered, his mobile face alight with pleasure as he saluted her with the glass of beer he was holding, flattered to see his creation disappearing so rapidly.

'Well, Meg,' Dan claimed Meg's attention, 'and what part of the old country are you from?'

For a long time he stayed with her, chatting easily, and she responded with all the pent-up need engendered by her isolation in Jasper Creek. Aware of strange vibes from Craig, who none the less scarcely spoke to her himself, she set out to enjoy herself, talking easily to Dan, laughing at his ready jokes as it gradually dawned on her that it was going to be great to have a male foil for the barbs that would come her way from Craig.

Alanna did not actually fly out until the following Friday, needing to stay around to tie up loose ends, to make sure that all her patients' records were up to date, to make visits to say goodbye to people, although she did stop work at the medical station to allow Dr McCormick to take over while she was still there on a consultation basis. Meg watched with interest to see how it was all arranged, noting the ease with which Dan moved back into the routine and with his woman friend in the village.

The change in her own living arrangement became very apparent abruptly on the Saturday morning when she had slept late and was awakened by the sound of a child's voice in the staff annexe. She had been in Chalmers Bay for two weeks. Lying in the warm bed, reluctant to move, she heard the high-pitched sound of a boy's questions. . . That would be Rob. Then she heard the murmur of Craig's deep voice, answering the boy. Then there were the tantalising smells of coffee and frying bacon. He was certainly losing no time in making himself at home now that the other bedroom was vacant. Quickly she got up and dressed in warm leggings and a shirt and sweater.

The boy was taller and thinner than when she had last seen him, Meg thought as she entered the sitting-room; not surprising, since it was well over a year.

'Hi. . .you're the nurse from Gresham,' Rob said as soon as he saw her, his thin, pale face lighting up under its thatch of fair hair. He paused in his task of going through their collection of music tapes and compact discs. 'Dad said you were here. I didn't believe him at first.'

'Hello, Rob. As unlikely as it seems, here I am! And here you are. That's even more unlikely, isn't it? Anyway, it's very nice to see you. Any more broken bones?'

'Nope.'

'Coffee, Miss Langham?' Craig appeared in the doorway of the kitchen. 'As you can see, I'm taking up residence.' He indicated a pile of bags and suitcases that had been deposited in the centre of the room. 'Since this is carnival weekend, I thought we'd do that first, then have the rest of the day free to enjoy the carnival. Dan's agreed to take call.'

'Why are you calling her Miss Langham?' Rob piped up, with the deadly perspicacity of the very young. 'You told me her name was Meg.'

'Yes. . .well, this is a work place.'

'Not here,' the boy said reasonably. 'This is where you live.'

'Your dad wants to keep me at arm's length,' Meg said, deciding to silence him with the truth, enjoying the exchange between father and son. 'Yes, Craig, I would absolutely love a cup of coffee,' she added sweetly, 'and while you're at it you might as well cook my breakfast too. The kitchen isn't big enough for the two of us.'

Rob would certainly have his uses, she thought; Craig would not risk showing himself up in front of the boy by being sarcastic to her.

'You're sure different from Gail,' Rob said wonderingly. 'She won't let Dad inside the kitchen at her place. He's a good cook, too. She doesn't wear any make-up like you do. . .and she isn't as pretty. She sure is bossy at school as well.'

'Yes, I expect I am different from her,' Meg agreed quietly, warmed by his pert comments, wondering whether Gail would keep Craig out of her bedroom too, assuming that he wanted to be in it. According to what Joyce Travers had told her all those months ago, it was highly likely that he did.

'I wish I could live here. I bet you're not bossy, are you?' Rob persisted.

'Well, no. . .I don't think I could be described as that,' she said soberly.

'Here's your coffee, *Meg*,' Craig said, pointedly emphasising her name, handing her a mug of aromatic coffee.

'Thanks. It must be somewhat—er—inhibiting having such an observant son,' she said.

'I know what "inhibited" means,' Rob said. 'It's true. . . He never kisses Gail, like he did some of the others.'

Meg burst out laughing, unable to help herself. 'I can see why Gail might be bossy with you, Rob,' she said, glancing over at Craig to see him looking at her stony-faced. The boy's unwitting humour was helping her to keep her sanity. He was giving her information too, unasked.

'Do you want to come to the carnival with us?' Rob

invited. 'She can come with us, can't she, Dad?'

'Well, I. . . No, I. . .' she began awkwardly.

'Dad. . .?'

'Sure. Come with us,' Craig said smoothly. 'Then we'll be together if there's a dire emergency back here. As for you, young man——' he turned to his son '—you be quiet and eat your breakfast. I'm getting just a little tired of the sound of your voice.'

At mid-morning the three of them, suitably clothed, let themselves out of the annexe, to be greeted by bright sunlight streaming from a clear blue sky. Such sunshine was appropriate for this Easter weekend of rebirth and renewal, for the coming celebration to the end of the darkness and extreme cold of winter. With her boots crunching on frozen snow, drawing in deep breaths of the pure air as she walked, Meg made her way slowly towards the pick-up truck that Craig had borrowed from the medical station to bring over his gear, slowing her pace to be with Rob, while his father walked just ahead of them, finding a path. It was too cold to walk to the centre of the village, to the open area in front of the Anglican church, which would be the hub of activity. There was to be a barbecue lunch served from the church hall, with caribou meat, hamburgers, hot-dogs and soup served with bannock. Probably a number of the local women would have baked cakes as well.

A few minutes later they were munching on steaming hot-dogs, which were cooling rapidly in their hands as they mingled with the crowd. A musical band, with an odd assortment of instruments, was playing on the enclosed porch of the church hall, the players muffled up to the eyeballs. There were ice sculptures lined up outside, waiting to be judged, some of surprising intricacy, with the proud artists hovering in the background; a side-street, off the main road, had been cleared of debris and set up for the start and end of the dog-sled races; teams of dogs were being assembled.

People yelled and called to each other, dogs yipped with excitement and impatience; the cacophony of sound from the band mingled with the whine and revving of skidoo engines. There was an atmosphere of heady euphoria, a sense of letting go. Even in the bitter cold that still prevailed, there was a sense that winter was really over.

As soon as Meg could manage it, when Rob's attention was engaged elsewhere, she gave them both the slip, disappearing easily into the jostling crowd. It was doubtful, she reasoned, that Craig really wanted her with him, having told her that he didn't give a damn what she did in her free time, so she certainly was not going to foist herself upon him. She would have a good time on her own.

It was not difficult to avoid them for a while, then when she next caught sight of Craig, having let her guard down somewhat, she saw him leaning casually against a woman who stood next to him; his crooked arm was on her shoulder in a gesture that was peculiarly intimate, Meg noted with a kind of sick recognition which stopped her in her tracks. Rob was there, with a little girl who looked slightly older than he was; that would be Gail's daughter, Meg surmised.

She hovered irresolutely a few yards behind them. For a couple who were not lovers, were 'just friends', according to Bonnie Mae, there seemed more in the easy alignment of their bodies in relationship to each other than mere camaraderie. Her throat tight with emotion, Meg felt a surge of hot jealousy, hating the feeling that she had proudly kept at bay until now where Craig was concerned. Heaven forbid that she would join the bitter coterie of has-beens who, according to gossip, peopled Craig's past; she recalled the hard, tight-lipped faces of Joyce Travers and Cynthia Parks as they had warned her off Craig. . .

Before Meg could turn away, to avoid them as she had intended, Gail half turned towards her to say something to Craig, so that Meg had a good view of her face. As Craig answered her, he moved his gloved hand slowly over her back to her hips in a gesture that seemed proprietorial. Yes. . .this was Gail Adamson. Meg could see the resemblance to the woman in the photographs that Joyce Travers had spitefully shown her. . . Gail had been on a boat then, in the summer, her long hair blowing in the wind, lifting up her face, eyes closed, to Craig to be kissed. . .a laughing, bronzed Craig.

Meg turned away quickly before they could see her, walking blindly back towards the church hall, with a sickening feeling of despair rising within her. Was Gail his kind of woman? She felt she knew enough about her now, second-hand, to be able to ask that question, if Joyce Travers could be believed. Come to that, was Craig her own kind of man, if that was even a valid question? All she knew at the moment was that he excited her beyond easy endurance. Again she chastised herself for ever coming to Chalmers Bay. . . She should have got out of it somehow.

It was obvious that Gail and Craig had certain aspects of their lives in common, as well as being very old friends. . .or perhaps lovers. There was a certain mystery about both of them. As much as Meg tried to quell her churning thoughts, so they came back to her like the beginning of an obsession.

Later she contrived to meet up with Craig and Rob again at the pick-up truck when it was time to go back, having kept an eye on it. Gail and her daughter had gone already.

'Where have you been?' Rob demanded of her

as soon as he saw her, while Craig looked at
her with eyes as cold as flint. 'You didn't meet Gail
and Cathy.'

'I thought you would all want to be together,' she
answered him brightly. 'Did you come here, up north,
because Gail was already here?' she asked Craig con-
versationally, reasoning that he would not snub her in
front of the boy.

At first she thought he was not going to answer her
as he paused to swing Rob up into the high cab of the
truck, displaying a gentleness and protectiveness that
was almost poignant. When the door was closed, he
said, 'Her presence was instrumental in my decision
to bring Rob here for a while. . .' There was a hard
edge to his voice. 'It's none of your business.'

Savagely he jerked open the door again and, before
she knew what he had intended, he had swung her up
beside the boy. 'Move over, Rob,' he said. The door
slammed.

Rob chatted all the way back to the annexe, oblivi-
ous, it seemed, to the fact that the two adults were
silent. Once there, he was immediately put to bed for
a nap in his father's room. He would go back to spend
the night at Gail's house.

Bonnie Mae knocked on the door and came in just
as Meg was wondering whether to go to her own room
or stay in the sitting-room with Craig. 'Hi there, you
two,' she greeted them, looking considerably different
and very attractive in casual clothing and a touch of
make-up. 'Just came to remind you guys that there's
a dance in the church hall tonight. Chuck's in town
for the weekend, so we're going.'

'I'm on call with Dan tonight, remember, Bonnie,'
Meg said. 'So it's out for me.'

'Oh, that doesn't matter. You can take the Bell Boy
beeper. And Dan will round you up if you're needed.

He's good at that. So you can take her, Craig. You're all set! No obstacles!'

There was an awkward silence to which Bonnie Mae seemed immune, while Meg looked everywhere but at Craig.

'Well,' Bonnie Mae said briskly, after a moment, 'we'll see you both there, then. Bye for now. It's a good thing for us to show up at community events.' Without elaborating further, she let herself out through the covered way.

There were no flies on Bonnie Mae, Meg thought ruefully as she walked stiffly into the kitchen, aware of Craig's presence with every fibre of her being. Scarcely aware of what she was doing, she began to clear up the few things they had left there from breakfast. Had Bonnie been aware of the animosity between them and deliberately provoked it? She knew that Bonnie Mae wanted everyone to be on good terms, and who could blame her? So far she had not informed Bonnie Mae of their past acquaintance. Her hands wavered at their task as she sensed Craig near her.

'That seems to be settled,' he said, with irony, managing to convey that she would be the last person he would choose. 'Rather than risk the wrath of Bonnie Mae. . .coming?'

'Well. . .' She stole a glance at him. His face was taut, expressionless. 'No. . .I don't think so.'

'Not even as a professional duty?' he said, mocking her. 'The antipathy is mutual, Miss Langham. . .even though we had a pretty good time at the last dance we were at, from what I remember.' They both stood very still. 'Don't worry, I'm not about to repeat the performance of what came after.'

Meg inhaled deeply, stung by the implied bitter rejection. 'OK, we'll put in an appearance. . .we'll do our duty! There's something I want to know first. What happened to Rob's mother?' There, she had said it! 'It's something I've wanted to ask you since I first saw him in the emergency department. He seemed so. . . so forlorn somehow. . .as though he needed a mother. I wondered then where his mother was. . .I mean. . .' Then she came to a verbal halt, suddenly appalled by her own questions, at what to him could seem like idle curiosity, or an attempt at a spurious intimacy. Perhaps she was subconsciously trying to provoke a confrontation with him, trying to clear the air, make him refute the rumours.

'I don't mean to pry,' she continued desperately, feeling that she would go mad if she didn't get some answers. 'It's just that I would feel more at ease with him if I knew. . .whether I could mention a mother.'

There was a loaded silence. Then Craig pushed his hands deep into the pockets of his thick corduroy trousers. He considered her broodingly, then shrugged. 'Rob's mother died of leukaemia about a year after he was born. . .about six months after she became ill. We weren't married. I officially adopted Rob as soon as we knew the diagnosis. . .we decided on that mutually. . .and that he would keep his mother's name. It's about all that's left of her. . .apart from him.'

'Why didn't you. . .didn't you. . .?' She hesitated, feeling herself getting into deep water.

'Marry her?'

'Yes.'

'I did ask her, when we knew she was ill. She didn't want it.'

'I. . .I see.'

'I doubt that you do,' he said, his tone weary, as though he was annoyed with her for having asked, but had decided to answer from an innate politeness. He was not, after all, a naturally boorish man, she knew.

It was a tone that did not invite confidence. 'At the time, I didn't understand myself, but I suspected. I prefer not to discuss it now. The need should not arise for you to mention her to Rob. He doesn't remember her; he was too young.'

'I'm sorry if I invaded your privacy,' she said, overcome by a new seriousness, a sadness, as she thought of the boy sleeping in the nearby room.

'Forget it! We'll go to the church hall after we've taken Rob back. Right?'

'Yes.'

In her room, sorting through her meagre wardrobe, she conceded that a weekend of ecstatic lovemaking with Craig last year did not give her a claim on him . . . no claim at all. Closing her eyes, she pressed her fingers against her tired lids. How on earth was she to get through the next few months?

CHAPTER FIVE

WHEN they walked towards the lighted entrance of the church hall, having taken Rob to sleep at Gail's house then parked the pick-up truck near by, they could hear the rhythmic pounding and chanting of an Arctic drum dance that Meg recognised from musical tapes she had listened to before coming to Chalmers Bay, but had not actually witnessed. Her tired senses quickened with excitement as she and Craig went through the door, drawn into the noise and warmth of the milling crowd inside. In a side-room they took off their outdoor clothing, exchanged their heavy boots for indoor mukluks, the soft skin boots.

There was an air of strange, electric excitement in the large hall as they went in to join the others. Meg searched the crowd for Bonnie Mae and Chuck as she and Craig were drawn into a long line of dancers who were moving slowly in time to the sound of the drums. Three elderly Inuit men were banging on the flat, plate-like drums of caribou skin which they held in their hands, chanting in their native language as they did so. The sound was picked up by singers all over the hall, rolling in waves of sound around them.

When that ended, other music of a more urban and modern type took over. Chuck, tall and bearded, dressed in a black and red check shirt and blue jeans, hailed them from across the room; he had his arms around Bonnie Mae, who wore a huge flowing caftan of brilliant colours underneath a heavy wool cardigan. Meg followed Craig as he forged a passage through the crowd to get to them. Introductions were shouted above the general din as Chuck's hand crushed Meg's diminutive one.

Blasts of cold air came in from time to time when someone opened the door, to penetrate the smoky, warm fug inside. There was no way that Meg could avoid dancing with Craig; everyone could see that they were together, would expect them to dance, so with a tenseness born of longing she went into his arms until the music was stopped and someone got up on the front stage to make an announcement in Inuktitut.

'What is he saying. . .any idea?' Meg asked Craig.

'I think they are using this dance as part of a wedding anniversary celebration, for a couple who have been married for a very long time. I can't make out all of it.'

A man and a woman, who appeared to be over eighty years old, obviously dressed in their very best clothes, were led on to the stage. At the same time, more drummers appeared with their characteristic flat native drums. When the first beats of the drums sounded, other people went up on the stage and began to dance in time to the beat. It was a slow, rhythmic, jerky dance of ritualistic movements in which, after a few moments, the elderly couple joined. The years seemed to drop off them as they moved, as though they had been born anew. Meg watched with fascination, feeling herself caught up in the generated emotion.

As she and Craig stood there in the centre of the room she became aware that some of the other dancers near them were forming a circle around them, facing in towards them, smiling, that other drummers appeared as though from nowhere. Then those near them, as well as on the stage, began to sing. . .a strange, lilting, haunting song, in the local language that she could not understand. It took her a few moments to realise that she and Craig were, like the old couple, the centre of a circle of attention.

'What are they singing? Is it for us?' She looked up at Craig enquiringly, a little afraid.

His face was both bemused and serious at the same time as he looked out over the circle of smiling faces. 'Yes, it's for us,' he said softly.

'What are they saying?' Involuntarily she moved closer to him, feeling her hand brush against his accidentally. Drawing back, she held herself aloof.

'They're saying that we. . .that we are ready for each other,' he said. There was laughter now in his voice.

'Ready. . .?'

'Yes,' he murmured, bending down close to her so that she could hear him above the rhythmic rise and fall of the sound. 'It's a wedding song.'

That admission must have been difficult for him, she thought wildly. She could not look at him. Ordinarily, in their former life, she might have laughed, attempted a witty rejoinder. So might he. Now her throat seemed to close up, to be gripped by a painful tightness. All the old repartee of University Hospital was irrelevant up here in the north. The lights in the room were dimmed; everyone around them was swaying to the poignant, evocative sound.

'They are saying that the long nights of darkness that remain before the summer are for us,' Craig translated. 'That the light of our love will be our sun. . .'

Meg stood stiffly beside Craig, suffering the physical contact as they were forced to stand close by the press of bodies, intensely sensitive to every part of him in this public place. Then, to her horror, she felt her eyes filling with tears. They were tears of yearning, drawn out by the song, for something that she could not have, something that these people seemed to know instinctively should be hers. Even in the very short time that they had both been in Chalmers Bay perhaps it was obvious to those around them that there was a certain something between them, that they were both of marriageable age and that it would be sensible for them to be together. But what about Gail, with whom he had been living? It was all very strange, having a surreal quality.

Then one of the men began to beat a drum again next to them. Perhaps he had seen the tears glittering in her eyes. Attention was diverted away from her and Craig as people began to dance the drum dance, still singing, moving in circles, stamping their feet, moving their arms in the prescribed movements that they had known for generations.

Meg turned away from Craig to plunge into the crowd. Frantically she made her way to the side-room where she had left her parka and snow pants, having an idea of taking the truck and driving back by herself. She had had enough of all this highly charged emotion. Unseeingly, automatically, she got dressed. What a fool she had been. . .was. . .to fall in love with someone who was not available. Not emotionally available, that was.

He was there blocking the way when she tried to leave. 'Why did you run?' he said.

'I want to drive back; I've had enough.'

'Wait for me,' he said, 'I've got the key to the truck.'

'Give it to me. There's no need for you to come.'

'You're upset. Why?' There was no one else in the room, which was piled with coats on tables and on the floor. Carefully Craig picked his way round piles of boots to get close to her.

'I. . .I felt we were here under false pretences. They thought that you and I. . .that we. . .' Meg found herself stammering. 'I don't know why.'

'It was a little teasing on their part, and a compliment. No need to take it so seriously. They see an unattached man and woman and they wonder why.'

'I think it was very serious,' she said.

'Does it matter? I know that we're not serious; that's all that matters. Any woman who could take off from Gresham the way you did obviously doesn't give a damn either.'

That's not true, she wanted to yell at him. 'I. . .I just felt. . .'

Unexpectedly he took her hand and kissed the backs of her fingers one by one, his lips warm against her cool skin. 'Calm down, Meg,' he said.

Then very slowly he turned her hand over and kissed the palm, then the soft inner skin of her wrist. The simple act was oddly, touchingly like an act of homage; it was intensely intimate. She watched as though it were happening to someone else. If she wasn't careful, he would see how besotted she was, and she mustn't let that happen, because he belonged to someone else, a woman who was no longer on this earth. . .and Gail.

'Let me take you back,' he said.

There did not seem to be anything that they could say as they drove back slowly over the snow, bumping and jolting, finally to come to a halt by the outer door to the annexe. Craig got out to help her down from the high cab of the truck.

'I'll put the truck away,' he said, his voice neutral.

'Thanks. I'm sorry I wasn't much in the mood for dancing. . .too tired, I guess.' Her voice trembled. 'Maybe Gail would like to go.'

'No. . .she's with the kids. She invited Greg Farley round to dinner. Get inside before you freeze.'

Wanting to be alone in the sanctuary of her room, Meg's hands became clumsy in her haste as she wrestled with the layers of heavy clothing in the warm sitting-room, with the boots that had become stiff with cold, thinking about his comment. Greg Farley, the RCMP officer, seemed to see Gail quite frequently. Didn't Craig mind?

Before she had got everything off, Craig was already in the room with her, removing his own outer gear, and had taken it all off when she still had one recalcitrant boot on.

'Let me do it,' he said with exasperation, as he might have said it to Rob. 'Sit here.' He indicated one of the wooden dining-chairs.

Silently she sat, holding out the foot with the boot on it, which Craig grasped at toe and heel with both hands as he knelt in front of her. When he gave a tremendous tug, the boot came off, bringing her three layers of socks with it. At the same time she slid off the chair and landed flat on her back, while the chair fell over with a thump.

'Aaggh. . .' She let out a cry, quite winded. She lay there panting, eyes closed. Then she felt his hands on her foot, massaging some life into it, warmly caressing.

'Your feet are freezing. . .'

When the movements stopped, she opened her eyes to find him looking at her, a searching look, unguarded. As though in slow motion he reached for her hands and pulled her to a sitting position so that her face was inches from his, so that she could feel the warmth that emanated from his body. Their eyes met, searching, waiting. . . She looked at the sensual curves of his mouth, parting her own lips in anticipation of his kiss, inviting him. . .

He accepted the invitation, touching his mouth tantalisingly to hers, then withdrawing, moistening her dry lips with his tongue so that her eyelids closed of their own volition and a sharp stab of desire quickened her already heightened senses.

'For God's sake, come here!' He capitulated, seeming to release his own iron will with a sigh as he pulled her against him, crushing her chest against his with one arm, holding her head with the other so that he could kiss her savagely, deeply. And she responded, twining her arms around his neck, digging her fingers involuntarily into his taut muscles, remembering how it had been on the night of the storm, knowing that once you had made love to a man fully it was not easy to call a halt, and she wanted him. . .

Soon she was murmuring assent when he touched her body, when he caressed her naked breasts, deliberately arousing her. Unashamedly she returned his touch, forgetful of everything but the feel of him. . .

The sound of a skidoo coming up to the medical station, very loud, caused them to pause. Craig was immediately alert. Like a cat, he got silently to his feet and padded over to a small window that gave a view of the main building, while she waited for him. Then, coming back to her, he pulled her to her feet.

'It's Bonnie Mae,' he said, 'coming back with Chuck. I envy their uncomplicated coupling. No hesitation. . . knowing exactly what they want.'

'How do you know they do?' she said.

After a moment, without replying, he swung her up into his arms and carried her into her room, putting her down just inside the door, which was wide open. Bending down to her level, he kissed her long and lingeringly, holding her forcefully against him, so that she was weak with compliance. Then he drew back.

'Goodnight, Meg,' he said quietly. 'I don't believe in happy ever after.' Before she could realise what was happening he had gone, leaving her standing there. He went to his own room and shut the door.

As she lay in bed later, with only her bruised lips and skin sore from the touch of his unshaven face to attest to the fact of their brief lapse, she remembered his earlier words: 'Now I wouldn't touch you with the proverbial barge pole', and 'Rob's mother died of leukaemia. . .'

CHAPTER SIX

IT WAS hardly surprising that Meg did not sleep well, that she woke long before it was time to get up, thinking of Craig so close to her physically yet seeming as far from her as he had ever been. When she got up to have a shower and dress for work she realised that she would not see as much of Craig as she had feared, or perhaps hoped. His schedule was different from her own; he and Dr McCormick would be coming to the medical station later in the mornings than she and Bonnie Mae would be; they would not clash at breakfast-time. Only the evenings might force them into each other's company somewhat, and even then he could leave to visit Rob or invite him over so that he and she would not be alone.

Monday, very busy, went by quickly. Meg ate her supper alone and went to bed early. Skip was already there when she went over to the outpatient area after breakfast on the Tuesday, where he greeted her with the news that he had only three more days to work before he would be leaving to go down south for several weeks to take some comprehensive nursing courses at the university in the city.

'You will certainly be missed here,' she said.

'Yes. . .well, I'm sure you will do just fine, Meg, when you have to take over. Anything you want to know about this place, you start asking now while I'm still here.'

When Bonnie Mae appeared and the patients began to arrive, work got under way. Dr McCormick came early, then Craig joined him. It was one of Meg's tasks to check the waiting-room in the clinic, to make sure that each patient was seen in sequence, to get out the appropriate record card from the files in the office, then find the patient's record folder. It was a simple, basic method. They did not yet need to use computers. She would then decide whether Dan or Craig should see a particular patient, trying to keep them equally busy. In between times, she helped Skip change dressings, or accompanied a doctor while a patient was being examined in one of the small cubicles. Bonnie Mae was the grand co-ordinator.

So far, she had been able to maintain her usual air of calm equanimity. . .at least, on the surface. Yet not for a moment could she forget Craig, there in actuality as well as in her inner awareness. As for Craig himself, he treated her in a professional manner, friendly and polite.

Just before lunchtime the waiting-room emptied. There would be an interval, then it would fill up again for the afternoon session. As Meg was tidying the desk in the office and thinking about taking a lunch-break, she heard the entrance door to the waiting-room open and close. Going to investigate, she found a young Inuit woman standing irresolutely in the centre of the room. The bonneted head of a young baby partially protruded from the back pouch of the *amauti* that the woman wore.

'Hello.' Meg smiled, hoping to put the woman at her ease. 'I'm the new nurse. Can I help you?'

'My baby is not well,' the woman said quietly, her eyes fearful. 'He throw up all the time. I'm so worried.' Little more than a child herself, she seemed too young to be in charge of a baby.

'Come with me.'

Inside one of the examination cubicles Meg lifted the baby out of the *amauti* and placed him on the examination table, where he immediately began to wail feebly. It was a thin, pathetic sound. In turn, the woman began to weep softly in sympathy and help-lessness.

'Undress him and cover him with this blanket,' Meg invited gently. 'I'll just get his birth and medical records. Tell me his name. And are you the mother?'

'Yes, I am his mother. His name is Jason Boucher,' the young woman whispered.

'OK, I'll be back in a moment, then we'll get things sorted out.'

The baby looked puny and dehydrated when she examined him a little later. Although one month old, he proved to weigh only a little more than he had weighed at birth.

'Are you breast-feeding him? And how often?'

'Yes, I am. Before. . .before this happened I was feeding him when he was hungry, at least five times in the day and sometimes at night. Now he seems hungry all the time. . .then he throw up and cry a lot. I don't know what to do.'

'When did that start?'

'About three days ago, but a bit before as well.' The young mother was fearful, looking apprehensively at Meg, then down at her baby whose thin arms waved above the blanket, his tiny hands balled into fists. 'The other nurse come to see me; she say the baby not gaining much weight. . .I did not tell her because maybe she think I do something wrong. . .not feed the baby right.'

'Does he have diarrhoea? Or a fever?'

'No. That is what I don't understand. He doesn't seem sick otherwise.' Self-consciously she wiped tears from her cheeks.

'When he vomits the milk after a feed, does it just sort of dribble out of his mouth, or does it come out more forcefully. . .sort of shoot straight out of his mouth?'

'Yes. . .yes, it comes out fast, a lot at once, suddenly.'

'I see,' Meg said. 'I'm going to take his temperature and pulse, listen to his heart, and take his blood-pressure. Then I'm going to get one of our doctors to look at him.'

'OK.'

Before Meg went to fetch Craig, she gently probed the baby's abdomen with the tips of her fingers. It sounded very much as though the problem was of a mechanical nature, an obstruction. Just as she had sus-pected, she could feel a small, firm lump, about the size of an olive, in the upper part of his abdomen.

Craig was in one of the other cubicles, so she lingered outside waiting for him.

'Want me?' he said on emerging. He was wearing the usual white lab coat over a green scrub suit, a uniform that somehow precluded any sort of intimacy, that seemed to put them both back in their professional places. Perhaps he was thinking the same thing as he quickly assessed her again from head to toe as she stood in front of him, trim in her pristine white uniform trouser suit.

'Yes.' She took a quick, deep breath, striving to be businesslike. 'There's a baby in cubicle two. He's one month old, been vomiting forcefully for three days, no obvious infection. I think he has a pyloric stenosis. . .I can feel something in his abdomen. I've made a few preliminary notes in the chart.'

'Mmm. Give me a minute, I'll be there,' he said.

'All right.'

The preliminary diagnosis that she had made proved to be correct as far as Craig was concerned. 'I congratu-late you, Meg,' he said quietly as his large, capable hands carefully pressed here and there over the baby's abdomen. 'What colour is the vomit?'

The mother answered, 'Sometimes it is like the milk, then sometimes it is light brown.'

'Mmm. That's probably a bit of partially digested blood. The stomach gets irritated and bleeds a little. What about his bowel movements—are they normal, would you say? For a breast-fed baby they should be quite yellow in colour, not too watery.'

'Um. . .no, more green.'

He turned to Meg. 'If we couldn't feel this moveable lump, we might have to send him south for a barium X-ray and maybe an ultrasound scan. As it is, I'm pretty sure you're right. We can get the mother to feed him a small amount, then we should be able to see the peristaltic movements of the stomach if he has a pyloric stenosis.'

Carefully Craig explained to the young mother that Jason had a pyloric stenosis, which was a narrowing of the outlet of the stomach, an over-growth of muscle, which prevented the stomach from emptying properly, hence the vomiting and pain. It usually developed for no apparent reason, he added.

As soon as he told her that the baby would need an operation, the woman began to sob. Meg put an arm around her shoulders, looking imploringly at Craig over her bent head, knowing exactly what she must be feeling. Never at ease herself with children in pain, because you could not explain disease to an infant, or why they felt pain, she tended to become emotional herself. Now she wanted to scoop the baby up in her arms and cuddle him, as well as comfort the distraught mother.

'It's all right,' she said. 'It's a simple operation, quite common. We could do it here at the medical station. Isn't that right, Dr Russell?'

'Yes, that's right, we could do it under local anaesthetic,' he agreed. 'I'd like to admit Jason immediately, because he's so dehydrated. When a baby vomits a lot he loses salt. That has got to be replaced, so we need to give him subcutaneous or intravenous fluid before we can operate. You can stay here with him, if you would like to. That would be the best thing for everyone concerned. Have you any other children, Mrs Boucher?'

'No, he is the only one.'

'That's good; you can be with him all the time, then.' Craig turned to Meg. 'Can you admit him and arrange for a bed for Mrs Boucher? Then I'd like to start subcutaneous glucose and saline right away, and put a stomach tube down. We could book the operation tentatively for tomorrow. This is a semi-emergency. We should have him rehydrated by then, his electrolytes OK.'

By the time the baby had been admitted and settled in a cot, with a bed for the mother beside it, Meg got a very late lunch-break. Baby Jason's mother returned home to collect an overnight bag and to let her family know what was happening. While she was gone, Craig inserted a fluid line in the baby's leg, and a thin stomach tube via Jason's nose. Meg asked Bonnie Mae to put a call through to Nuna, the nursing aide, to ask if she could come in that evening to work the night shift to supervise the baby.

At last, after handing over to Skip, who was also having to run the afternoon clinic, Meg hurried back to the annexe to get herself some lunch. As well as being ravenously hungry, she felt light-headed from lack of sleep. Already she felt as though she had been at the medical station for months.

Baby Jason was hungry but no longer dehydrated by the following morning. Dan McCormick, who had

slipped easily into the routine of the medical station
that was so familiar to him, agreed with Craig that
they would use a local anaesthetic and a sedative for
the baby and he would assist Craig.

'It's quite a while since I did a pyloromyotomy,'
Craig admitted as he carefully swabbed the sedated
baby's abdomen with an antiseptic solution at the start
of the operation.

'Well, Craig,' Dan quipped, 'if you find you can't
cope, I'll take over.'

Craig chuckled. 'I'm sure Skip will pounce on me
with advice if I dare to hesitate for more than two
seconds, eh, Skip?'

'Right on, Dr Russell!'

'And what about you, Meg? Are you going to
pounce on me?' His astute eyes met hers probingly
over the edge of his face mask.

'I. . . Actually, I've never seen a pyloromyotomy,'
she said quietly, lowering her eyes to watch his deft
hands as he placed sterile drapes over the tiny, inert
form of the baby.

'Well, to refresh your memory, I'm going to make
a small incision in the upper abdomen, locate the lower
end of the stomach, at the pyloric sphincter, find the
over-growth of muscle, then simply make an incision
in it to release the muscle fibres, right down to—but
not through—the inner lining of the canal. That will
get rid of the obstruction, after which the stomach will
be able to empty normally.'

'Now you're talking like a general surgeon,' she
answered him, not doubting for one moment that he
knew precisely what to do. Coming to the north frequently as he did, he was able to maintain a certain
level of expertise in all types of surgery.

The operation went smoothly and quickly. Bonnie
Mae left them to it while she got on with other things.

In no time at all, it seemed, Jason was in the recovery-room waking up from the anaesthetic with Meg watching over him, while Craig went to the ward area to see Jason's mother.

On the long stretcher the baby was such a tiny scrap of humanity that her heart went out to him and she stroked his downy hair away from his forehead as he made a few whimpering noises, gagging slightly on the rubber airway that was in his mouth to ensure a clear passage of air. From now on he would be able to take his milk without vomiting, would rapidly put on weight over the next few weeks. They would keep him as an in-patient for at least several days, then someone from the medical station would visit him regularly at home.

'Wake up, Jason,' she whispered, stroking his soft cheek, bending close. 'All over, sweetheart.' There was a desire in her to communicate with him. Although he would not understand her words, perhaps he would be soothed by the sound of her voice as he was waking up.

'I wish you would call *me* sweetheart, Meg,' Dan spoke behind her.

'Oh, yes?' she smiled up at him, 'If you were Irish I'd say you'd kissed the blarney stone.'

He laughed. 'The little fellow's looking good. We have to guard against gastro-enteritis now; everything that goes into his stomach must be sterile. We have to educate the mother. I'll get Bonnie Mae to do that. She has the right—er—overbearing persona, wouldn't you say? "You do this, or else". . .'

'Yes, you're right.' Meg smiled again, feeling very relaxed with him, just as Craig entered.

'How's he doing?' Craig asked her, frowning.

'Fine. I was just thinking of taking out the airway.'

'Wait a little longer. Leave him attached to the monitor for a while. I'll be back later.' He made a quick assessment of Jason, then moved to the doorway. 'Dan, there are a few things on which I want to confer with you.'

'OK, lead on!'

When they had gone, Meg swallowed a nervous lump in her throat. Now she fully understood the old adage about the inadvisability of mixing business with plea- sure, which she had more or less adhered to up till now. Chalmers Bay was not the sort of place where one could stick to such good intentions easily. Resolutely returning to business, she began to chart Jason's vital signs. Most likely, if all went well, he would be able to go home as early as Sunday. They would all have to assess how well the mother could cope.

By Friday evening Jason was feeding from his mother. Meg had taught her how to aspirate the con- tents of the stomach with a syringe, via the stomach tube, if Jason looked as though he was going to vomit, which he could do while the operation site was healing. By taking small amounts of milk at a time, very fre- quently, he was managing to keep it down. Soon they would be able to remove the stomach tube.

Back in her room late that evening, having handed over to Nuna, Meg hoped fervently that they would have a quiet weekend. Her need for adequate sleep was desperate. Skip would be flying out this weekend, weather permitting. Without him, the two nurses would deal with everything, including little Jason, with the invaluable help of Nuna. As she and Bonnie Mae had discussed the hours that they would be able to take off, Bonnie Mae had made the succinct comment, 'You'll spend two-thirds of your time working, the other third sleeping—if you're lucky—or under the shower.'

CHAPTER SEVEN

As EACH day dawned, there was a barely perceptible easing of the frigid temperatures. However unpredictable the weather, from a quick, vicious storm to a day of surprising, opalescent beauty, it was inevitable now that the summer would come, when for a brief period the tundra would be green with frantically growing things and the air would be replete with the sounds of migrating birds coming home to breed.

Baby Jason, recovered, was discharged home, where he had to be visited frequently to make sure that the young parents could cope, that they were being supervised by a grandmother. Adele James had come up to have her stitches out and was now waiting for the final lab report.

Meg began to make house calls on her own, taking the skidoo to visit those patients who had become familiar to her by first coming to the medical station, while Bonnie Mae generally dealt with the old familiars. They learned to compensate for the absence of Skip, which considerably cut down on her and Bonnie Mae's free time.

Tommy Patychuk came one day to have some scars on his legs loosened up by being cut here and there, what Craig called 'revision of scars'; Meg helped him do it in the outpatient department, using local anaesthetic.

Living with Craig was proving less traumatic than she had expected, since they often did not see a great deal of each other when they were not actually working together. On the fourth weekend after her arrival, Rob

111

was over with them for the two days, as he often was
now, which meant that they were inevitably getting to
know each other well. He was an intelligent, sweet-
natured boy, with a sharp sensitivity to human nuances.

'Will you read me a story, Meg?' he announced on
the Friday evening, having been put to bed on the
small sofa in the sitting-room where he was going to
spend the night as a special treat, after what had been
a strangely amicable and intimate evening, just the
three of them. Craig had been unusually quiet and
amenable while they had eaten together, had listened
to his son chattering to Meg.

'Well, I'm afraid we haven't got any suitable books
here,' she replied thoughtfully. 'I could possibly tell
you one, from memory,' she added, racking her brains
to think of stories from her childhood. 'The only ones
I usually remember begin with "once upon a time"
and end with "happily ever after".'

Even as she heard herself uttering those words, she
recalled ruefully that they were the very words that
Craig had spoken to her so recently. 'I don't believe
in happily ever after,' he had said. As she felt her
cheeks grow pink with embarrassment, she strove to
hide her gaffe by carrying plates into the kitchen.

As she passed Craig, he looked up at her from his
chair. 'That figures,' he said softly. She did not look
at him.

'That's all right,' Rob called after her. 'I like those
stories best.'

'All right, then,' Meg said, coming back into the
room and seating herself beside Rob. 'Let me
think. . .' Her eyes met Craig's as he looked at her
over the top of the newspaper he held. His expression
was one of sardonic amusement. Pursing her lips and
averting her eyes, Meg made a lightning choice from
her limited repertoire of remembered stories.

'Once upon a time,' she began in a determined tone, 'there was an old wood-cutter who lived in the middle of a deep, dark wood. . .'

A muffled snort of laughter from behind the newspaper interrupted her thought processes, so that she paused. Craig got up and left the room.

The idyll of family life came to an abrupt end on Saturday, when they had to deliver two babies. One of the women was able to go home with her baby, while the second, who was slightly toxic, had been advised to stay in for a night or two, which mean that Nuna would have to come in for the night shift and Meg would have to be there in the late evening.

Dan McCormick was the one on call. 'Hi, Meg.' He came in near the end of her shift to see the mother and baby, looking relaxed and casual. 'How's it going?'

'Fine,' she assured him. 'Her blood-pressure's OK, no excessive bleeding, and the baby is perfect.'

'Good. I'll be going home now. Nuna has my number if I'm needed. It's Bonnie Mae on call for the night with me, isn't it?'

'Yes.'

'Craig said to tell you that he's at Gail's place, in case you wonder where he is. He'll be back at the annexe later. Goodnight, Meg.'

''Night, Dan.' With a superhuman effort, Meg kept her face neutral as Dan saluted her from the doorway before disappearing, then felt her features change into something like a mask of despair once she was alone.

While she waited for Nuna, she tried to reread a long letter she had picked up from the post office that day. It was from a good friend of hers, Jen, who had worked with her in the emergency department and then in the OR in Gresham, telling her that staff were needed at a new day-surgery unit at the hospital and suggesting that she should apply. Although Jen's proposal was very tempting, it was probable that she would find herself working with Craig again for some of the time. Did she want that? Jen also told her that her former head nurse, Joyce Travers, had been promoted since Meg's departure to an administrative position, then had been made redundant shortly after, news that gave Meg a sense of vindication. It was Joyce Travers who had seen Craig give her that quick, unsolicited kiss in the prep-room in the OR, and it was Joyce who had waylaid her later and said to her in a vicious tone, 'You don't think Dr Russell cares about you, do you?' Without waiting for a reply, she had gone on, 'If you do, you're greener than I thought. . .and you're about as green as they come.'

Meg had been shocked by the rancour in that verbal attack and had gone about her work in a numb state for the rest of that day, scarcely consoled by the insight that Joyce must harbour frustrated feelings for Craig herself. It was then that she had made a vow of sorts not to join the queue. Later, another colleague, Cynthia Parks, who had seen her and Craig get into Craig's car on the night of the storm, had also commented, 'Be careful of him. . .he's a heart-breaker!'

'Are you speaking from personal experience?' she had asked, exasperated by this unasked-for advice.

Cynthia had merely flushed and given an emphatic, 'No!'

Joyce Travers had certainly not let it rest either; she had been the one instrumental in Meg's decision to leave Gresham quickly, even going as far as showing Meg photographs of Gail and Craig together on a boat during a hospital party. 'That's Gail Adamson,' Joyce had told her. 'Her marriage broke up because of Craig Russell. . .she was a friend of his son's mother. If there's going to be another Mrs Russell, it will be her.'

Joyce had enjoyed saying that, and Meg had got up quietly, handed her back the photographs, and said pointedly, 'I understood there never was a Mrs Russell.' Then she had walked out of the staff coffee-room with the feeling that she had well and truly cooked her goose with the head of her department.

When she heard Nuna's footsteps approaching the ward area she was ready to leave.

'Meg. . . Meg. . .' Nuna said urgently as she arrived, coming into the office area of the recovery-room and dumping her bag. 'There's a search party being organised in the village right now. A young girl's missing. . . seems to have walked out on the tundra and not come back. She's been gone since this morning. Her father and the RCMP are getting up the search.' She paused for breath. 'They were wondering if someone from here could join the search, in case she's hurt, you know. . .if they find her, that is. . .'

'Why did she go?' Meg ran a hand tiredly through her hair, fearing the answer. It was not uncommon that some of the local young people suffered from depression during the angst of growing up, then sought drastic measures. It had been the same at Jasper Creek.

'She's very depressed, so the family say. First, her boyfriend went down south to college, then her mother went away to the city three weeks ago to have an operation. The girl, Anik, thinks that her mother has died and no one wants to tell her. It's not true, but she hasn't heard from her mother since the day after she got there. Anik's a quiet girl. . .she doesn't say much, but she thinks a lot. She's only fourteen. . .she still needs her mother.'

'That's very sad. Couldn't she speak to her mother by telephone?'

'She did on the day after she got to the city, then nothing. Poor girl!'

'What can I do?' Meg offered, feeling some of her tiredness lift.

'You could take the small emergency kit, take the skidoo to the RCMP headquarters. . .that's where the search is taking off from. Find out where they want you to go. Don't go by yourself, whatever you do. Go with someone who knows the tundra. Take the big flashlight that's with the kit. It's better if you go, then Bonnie Mae will be here for any emergencies. See what Bonnie Mae says first.'

'Yes, I'll call her in her quarters.'

Fifteen minutes later, in her heavy outdoor gear, with the emergency box strapped behind her on the skidoo, Meg made her exit from the garage at the medical station, driving cautiously. The single brilliant light at the front of the skidoo slashed a swath through the dark night, revealing the hard, frozen snow in her path. As she turned the nose of the machine towards the centre of the village, as she braced herself against the onslaught of the sharp cold, gripping the wide handlebars, a feeling of sick anticipation engulfed her.

CHAPTER EIGHT

BEFORE she reached the area where the RCMP head-quarters were situated, Meg could see milling lights, and what looked like the entire adult population of Chalmers Bay swarming around the building on the packed snow. There was a kind of suppressed tension and anxiety in the atmosphere.

Meg steered the skidoo to the side of the main build-ing and parked it there among others. With the heavy emergency box in one hand, she moved closer to the action. Some people were starting up their vehicles, heading out towards the dark tundra. In the light thrown from the porch of the police headquarters she recognised Greg Farley, holding a clipboard and directing searchers. Meg hung back, anonymous in her parka. It would be necessary for her to pair up with at least one other person; she had no idea where to go or what to do.

'Hi! You are Meg?' Someone touched her arm. A slight figure stood beside her, dressed in a *qulittaq*, a caribou-skin parka, and in the circle of light from the flashlight that he carried she recognised Tommy Patychuk. With him were two large husky dogs, their coats thick and lustrous. 'You are part of the search?'

'Hello, Tommy. Yes, I'm Meg. I'm glad to see some-one I know. I don't know whether I can be of much use.'

'You come with me,' he said. 'We have to let the RCMP know our route and we must not deviate from that, otherwise a lot more people get lost. I think I know where Anik might be. . .a place she used to go with Tarsis, her boyfriend. . .I have told them, but they do not think she will be there, because someone saw her walking in a different direction. I know Anik very well; she is my friend.' The boy spoke earnestly, with a calm assurance. 'I know the way she thinks. She was depressed; I think she wanted to go to a place where she could feel close to Tarsis and to her mother, where she and her mother used to fish in the summer when she was a little girl, when her mother was well. I feel she will be there, near the big *inukshuk* that has stood for as long as anyone here can remember.'

'What's an *inukshuk*?' Would it be wise, Meg considered, to go with this boy? How great was the possibility that they might both get lost looking for the girl? But something about his certainty moved her to trust in him as he stood quietly with his dogs.

'A pile of stones and rocks as big as a man, or two men, that is built as a marker on the land so that others might know where they are and not be lost,' the boy explained. 'If Anik is out on the tundra, she will have built an igloo. She is a very clever girl.'

'You mean that we should go together, just the two of us?'

'Yes. We would take a dog team and a *qamutik*— a big wooden sled that belongs to my grandfather. Come.' Taking her arm, Tommy drew her away from the crowd that was rapidly diminishing as more searchers mounted their skidoos and moved off. 'These two dogs are mine; my father has three dogs and my grandfather has two more, which will make seven. With seven dogs we can make good speed.'

'What does your family think of this? You are very young,' Meg said carefully.

'My aunt thinks I should go, so does my grandfather. I have much experience and they trust me. My father has already left on the search, with two skidoos and

three other men. I like dogs better; they can scent. . .
they know the way home. You wish to come with me?
I am fifteen, no longer a child.' The boy stood proudly,
waiting for her reply.

'Yes.' Meg made up her mind quickly, before her
better judgement could raise all sorts of objections.

'I'm glad you will come,' he said. 'The route is
simple. It will be along by the Gulf, more or less in a
straight line, except here and there where we will have
to come inland a little to avoid some big rocks.' As
he talked they moved quickly in the direction of the
house that Tommy's aunt shared with his grandfather.
Having made the decision to go, they now felt a sense
of urgency.

'Why did everyone wait until night to search for the
girl, if she's been missing all day?' Meg panted as
they hurried along, with Tommy being pulled by the
energetic dogs.

'The family thought she was at a friend's place, then
when they found that she wasn't there someone
reported that they had seen her walking out on to the
tundra in the morning, carrying a rifle, and had not
come back. She is a good shot, so she will not have
been eaten by a polar bear.'

In spite of his assertion about Anik's prowess with
a gun, Meg detected fear in his voice. Perhaps the girl
meant more to him than a friend; perhaps he saw the
absent Tarsis as a rival. There was an intensity about
him, a determination to find Anik at all costs, that
communicated itself to Meg.

'OK,' she said firmly. 'Let's get going, Tommy, as
fast as we can.'

'Right! Here's the shed where I have the other dogs.'

They had come to Charlie Patychuk's house. As they
approached the shed, the two dogs who were with
them started to bark furiously, echoed by barking in

the interior of the shed. Five dogs darted out when the door was dragged open, barking, yipping and leaping. Beside the shed was the big wooden sled, already packed with boxes covered by a tarpaulin to form a secure seat between them and to protect whatever supplies Tommy had there.

While the dogs leapt and snarled at each other in good-natured rivalry, Tommy prepared to harness them. 'I'm going to use a fan hitch,' he said. While Meg watched, fascinated, he attached a harness quickly and expertly to each dog, then clipped each one to the wide fan hitch that was attached to the front of the *qamutik*, admonishing the dogs sharply if they became too boisterous or refused to stand still.

'This is Nanook,' Tommy said, introducing the lead dog, talking as he worked. 'It means polar bear in Inuktitut. Females make the best lead dogs; the males will run after them and will not fight so much.'

Indeed, the beautiful dog deserved the name. Her fluffy hair was a very pale silvery grey, tipped with white. She held herself proudly as she waited at the head of the team with controlled impatience in every line of her body, longing to run. The other dogs continued to yap and pant around her, wild with excitement.

Tommy went inside the house briefly and came out with a caribou-skin parka of the type that had to be pulled on over the head, with a wide, deep hood, and the fur on the inside. 'This is for you,' he said, offering her the garment. 'Please put it on over your own parka. The tundra will be very cold.'

She did as she was told.

'Would you sit here, Meg, between these two boxes, under this caribou-skin rug, so that you will not fall off the sled? And please, I will need you to hold the light steady so that we can see where we are going. I shall stand behind at the push bar to command the dogs. We are ready.'

With flashlight switched on, the light sparkling on the packed, frozen snow ahead of them, Meg waited for the next move, with her eyes on the magnificent dog, Nanook, who had braced herself for the imminent take-off.

Tommy spoke to the dogs sternly in his own language, no doubt admonishing them to behave themselves, then he gave a sharp whistle. In unison, as though with one exultant voice, the dogs began a wild barking as they leapt forward, tails waving aloft, pulling the heavy sled as though it weighed next to nothing. As they gathered speed the barking died down, each dog concentrating on the task in hand. They were working dogs; they lived to run.

Less than fifteen minutes later they were on the edge of the village near the airstrip, having reported their route to the authorities, heading west in the direction of a distant *inukshuk*. As the last lights of human habitation, human warmth and help, moved swiftly to the rear with each straining pull of the dogs, Meg hunkered down in her unlikely seat, covered with a heavy caribou-skin rug that enclosed her like a sleeping-bag. Then human beings and dogs plunged with hope into the black night.

'Here we go!' Tommy called to her. Then with high, ringing cries he urged the team to even greater efforts. 'Hi, hi, hi, hi, hi!'

Now that they were at the point of no return, Meg found herself questioning whether she should have come on the search in case she was not back in time for any work tomorrow. But it was a short-lived questioning. Her concentration reverted to keeping the wavering beam of light over the backs of the straining dogs to the tundra beyond so that they were not run-

ning blindly. This was all that mattered at the moment.
Meg forgot the discomfort and cold of the *qamutik* as
she was buffeted from side to side between the boxes.
Their thoughts were on a girl. . .a sweet, shy girl who
had talked herself into thinking her mother was
dead. . .a girl out at night on the wild, lonely tundra.
All their hopes were pinned on finding her alive.

'*Howa-ii*,' Tommy called to the dogs, the sound of
his voice dying away swiftly in the vastness. Obediently
the dogs turned to the right, towards Coronation Gulf.
The runners of the sled made a dull, crunching sound
that mingled with the laboured breathing of the dogs.
'Now we must be alert,' the boy said to Meg. 'We
must watch out for her. Every so often we will stop
to call for her; sometimes we shall light a fire so that
she can see the flames and smell the smoke. She may
see the light from our sled.'

'What if she does not want to see?' The fear had to
be voiced.

'She will want to. . . She will know that we love her.'

There had been nothing in her life up to now that
could compare with the physical thrill of being on a
dog-sled, Meg decided as small slivers of frozen snow
from the dogs' racing feet stung her face. She was
quickly disabused of the idea, too, that one had to yell
'Mush!' to get a dog team going, even though Tommy
could rightfully be called a 'musher'.

The speed at which they were travelling was amazing, gauged by the landmarks of small hillocks of frozen
snow on either side of them which seemed to fly past.
Tommy had to be constantly alert, to call to the dogs to
turn quickly either right or left before they encountered
obstacles that appeared in the powerful beam of the
light, wavering like glimmering ghosts. It was then that
his skill was very apparent.

'*Hulla*,' he shouted, for the team to turn left, then,

'*Howa-ii*,' for them to turn right. They lost all sense of time on the swaying, lurching vehicle.

'Who-a-a!' The long-drawn-out cry brought the dogs to a reluctant stop when they had been travelling for what seemed like ten minutes. Tommy jumped off the back of the sled to anchor it with a snow-hook, like a steel claw. Apparently, the dogs were not so disciplined that they would not run off. As Meg directed the light, Tommy ran to the front of the sled to place a similar hook there.

'One of us must always stay with the sled,' he said. 'Now I want to call for Anik. Up ahead there are some big rocks that we must go round, so we must turn to the left, then later we must turn to the right again to resume our course. I do not think she will be here, but we should not go on without making sure. Please shine the light for me; I want to make a small fire so that she will see us if she is here.'

Heaving herself out of the warm cocoon of the caribou-skin rug, Meg stepped down carefully. If the dogs were to take off now, they would be marooned. As she hung on to the push bar of the sled and directed the light, Tommy emptied the contents of a small box on to the snow a short distance from the sled, poured a little kerosene on the pile and set it alight. When the flames roared up, consuming pieces of wood and what looked and smelled like bits of old rubber boots, a wide circle of white was illuminated, edged with impenetrable darkness. It was easy to imagine wolves or polar bears lurking at the edge, padding silently just beyond her vision. Meg shivered. She did not think there were really wolves quite this far north; in any case, they seldom attacked humans, although the bears were an ever-present, dangerous reality.

Then Tommy began to call, turning slowly in different directions, cupping his hands around his mouth to contain the sound. 'Anik! Anik! Anik!.' When he turned to the west, towards the towering rocks which he had said were there ahead, which they could not yet see, his cries echoed back to them mournfully like the cries of disembodied spirits. 'Ik! Ik! Ik!'

For the first time, Meg felt the stab of a primitive fear, physical and very immediate, coming as it did with the knowledge that a mistake in this environment, a wrong judgement, could mean death. And who was she to make such judgements? The very land around them seemed to take on a quality of sentience, as though it were alive. . .waiting, watching. It was not menacing, just unequivocally powerful.

The acrid scent of the burning rubber filled her nostrils as the thick smoke wafted towards her. If Anik was anywhere in the area she would surely smell it too. When Tommy began to call again, she joined him, as though their puny voices could take on the vastness of the landscape. 'Anik! Anik! Anik!'

Please, please answer! Meg willed the silence to answer them as she felt a similar, tense will in the boy beside her. 'Ik! Ik! Ik!' Only the mocking sound of the echo returned to them.

With the echo this time, the dogs began to bark, continuing for several minutes, stirring restlessly in their harness. Then, inexplicably, Nanook sat down, lifted up her beautiful head towards the sky, showing her soft white throat, flattened her ears, and let out a long, answering howl, a wail of undulating, primal sound.

Before the sound had come to an end, its echo reached them, as though from a wolf waiting in the wings, so that the other dogs joined in one by one until there was a cacophony of sound, moving out, bouncing back.

Transfixed to the spot where they stood, Meg and

Tommy remained perfectly still. Louder than any sound they could have made, the dogs seemed to be sending out their own message to the lost girl. If blood could curdle in human veins, it was doing so now; Meg felt an odd sensation of tingling within her body, a reaction as instinctive as it was ancient. Let the girl still be alive. . .please. . .she found herself praying.

For minutes the sound went on and on. An intuitive feeling came to Meg that the girl was not in this spot, as Tommy had also thought, but that she was somewhere further on. . .that she could perhaps hear the calling of the dogs. An impatience to continue the search gripped her, yet she dared not move, as though they were in the throes of a spell that could not end until the dogs were silent.

Nanook lowered her head, stood up abruptly, gave herself a little shake. One by one the other animals stopped their wailing and stood up too. A collective restlessness took over, as though a wind had passed over them.

Tommy broke the silence that had descended. 'It is time to go,' he said quietly, calmly. 'She is not here.'

As though nothing at all had happened, the dogs turned prosaic gazes on the two humans who prepared to mount the *qamutik*. There was something just a little superior in that regard, albeit an encompassing, friendly superiority.

Three more times they stopped in the same manner, lit a fire, called out in unison over the barrens. Each time the tension and anxiety increased when no response came, as well as the impatience to get to the *inukshuk*, which was very close now; they knew that the girl could not have walked further than that. They crouched by the fire until it died down, absorbing what precious warmth they could now that the night chill was penetrating their clothing. What if the boy was

wrong about where Anik might have headed? Meg
allowed the thought to come to the forefront of
her mind.

'Not far now,' Tommy said, perhaps sensing the nig-
gling doubt in her mind. 'When we get there we shall
drink some hot chocolate that I have brought with us,
and some brandy.'

'Great!' She stood up decisively. 'Let's go!'

The stone sentinel, as the boy had said, was as tall as
two men. It loomed up suddenly, directly ahead of
them, looking at once reassuring and sinister, as it
appeared indistinctly in the wavering yellow light from
the flashlight that Meg held. As they neared it, she
could see that it was made of varying-sized pieces of
flat rock that were piled one on top of the other on a
double base, to form a sturdy column that would not
be toppled by the wind that kept it stripped of snow.
Generations ago, someone had built this as a monu-
ment and marker, on the top of a hillock.

'Whoa-a-a!'

Once again they came to a halt, dismounted,
anchored the sled. This time there was a desperate
hope in both of them, because this time they would
be turning back if there was no response. Neither one
of them had voiced the question of how long they
would stay here, how long they would keep trying
before giving up in defeat.

'Let's get the fire going, Tommy, and have
that drink.'

'What we will do after,' he said, 'is make a search
of the area in widening circles until we have covered
all this area around the *inukshuk*. . .until we have
decided that she is not here. . .' His voice wavered
and died, so that Meg impulsively wrapped her arms
around him in a tight hug.

'Yes, we'll do that. Come on. . .'

The hot chocolate, poured from a vacuum bottle, was the most wonderful thing she had ever tasted, thick and sweet. They stood next to a blazing fire to drink it while they contemplated the next move. If the girl had come this far on foot, it would be in this vicinity that she would have built an igloo for shelter. She would have brought with her the large curved snow-knife that was used to cut blocks of frozen snow for an igloo.

There was no sound here other than the laboured, raucous pants of the tired dogs, who lay flat out on the snow now, their sides heaving. Presently, when they were rested, Tommy would feed them chunks of frozen caribou meat, just enough to keep them going for the return journey.

Thoughts of Craig intruded, insinuated themselves into Meg's mind as she strained her eyes to penetrate the darkness beyond the circle of fire, and a loneliness pervaded her, a memory of how he had kissed her fingers. She wished he were here now with her. Did he know, have any idea, where she was? Would he care?

'Please, Meg, I would like you to shine the light for me while I walk a little way off and fire a gun so that Anik will hear it, if she is here.' As he spoke, Tommy stowed the food and drink and uncovered a rifle from the sled. 'I do not want to frighten the dogs. I shall walk maybe fifty yards. OK?'

'OK.' Walking to the edge of the circle of light thrown by the fire, she shone the beam of the flashlight into the darkness towards the frozen water of the Gulf, keeping Tommy within the beam as he walked away from her carrying the gun. At the very end of the light, he lifted the rifle towards the sky and fired.

Instantly the dogs were on their feet, barking furiously with a renewed energy, so that Meg feared they

might pull the snow-hooks from their anchorage and
disappear with their sled into the night. 'Hurry up,
Tommy,' she called to him in a voice that was high-
pitched with fear.

They waited tensely then, both for the dogs to be
silent and for any answering signal, standing side by
side for comfort. As the barking ceased, a small wind
sprang up, moaning softly around the stone sentinel,
ruffling the coats of the dogs. Tommy pushed back his
hood, to reveal a woollen hat underneath, so that he
could hear better. Without comment, Meg did the
same, straining to hear something other than the wind
as she moved her head slowly this way and that.
Minutes passed.

A single gunshot, at a distance and in front of them,
rent the air, causing the dog team to erupt again in a
frenzy of noise.

'It must be Anik! It must be!' Tommy turned to
Meg, his face alight with joy and excitement, shouting
above the exultant barking. Simultaneously they flung
their arms around each other in a triumphant hug. Meg
kissed him on the cheek and saw that he was crying.
Although they had known each other such a short time,
it seemed natural that in adversity and triumph they
should comfort each other.

'Quick, Tom, let's put more on the fire. . .the kerosene! Where is it?'

'OK. . .' He was laughing and crying at the same
time, with whimpering, relieved sobs. 'It must be
her. . .'

'Careful, careful. . .don't set yourself alight with
that stuff! The wind could blow it over us.' She dashed
tears away from her eyes with the back of her heavy
gloves before they could freeze on her cheeks, then
carefully poured more kerosene from a can at the edge
of the fire. As the flames flared up anew, they stepped

back and both began to shout, the vapour from their breath visible in the air.

'Anik! Anik! Over here!'

It was doubtful that the girl could hear their calls above the near-demented noise of the dogs, who were straining in their traces towards the source of the sound they had heard. From that straining, it was possible to pin-point the direction of the shot.

While Tommy moved agitatedly from one foot to another, waiting impatiently, Meg swung the light over the snow beyond the glow of the fire, praying that the noise they were making would frighten away any polar bears, rather than attracting them.

'She could be hurt,' Tommy shouted to her. 'If she does not get here in about five minutes, we must take the team and look for her. Stay close to me and the gun, Meg, in case there are bears. Keep alert.'

'Yes, OK.'

The moment the sound from the dogs diminished, the boy shouted again, 'Anik, it's Tommy. . .Tommy Patychuk!' Turning to Meg, he said, 'She may be frightened to come if she does not know who it is, in case someone will be mad with her for coming out here, for causing trouble.'

Scarcely daring to breathe, they waited. With the rifle clenched firmly in his right hand, Tommy moved close to Meg, grasping her arm with his left hand, as though sensing an approach from someone, person or animal.

It was Meg who saw her first, a darker shadow in the darkness, just outside the circle of light, motionless. 'There she is,' she whispered, pointing, her nerves at breaking-point.

The boy ran forward without hesitation. As he did so, the other figure moved forward also, hesitantly at first, then with more assurance. They spoke in

Inuktitut briefly before throwing their arms around each other, while Meg stayed back, scanning the darkness, lest their utter relief at finding the girl should overshadow their caution about other dangers.

Anik, who was about the same height as Tommy, was bashful and shy when Tommy led her over to Meg. Briefly she lifted a tear-stained, childlike face to look at Meg, then hung her head down dejectedly. She wore a caribou-skin parka which had a hood trimmed with wolf fur and she carried a rifle.

'I suggest we get back to Chalmers Bay as quickly as possible,' Meg said, feeling that it was about time she asserted some authority that was in keeping with her adult status, 'so that the search can be called off. We should eat something quickly. . .if we're safe here.'

'Anik has an igloo just over there.' Tommy pointed. 'We can take the sled over; I can stake out the dogs for a few minutes while we go inside to eat. I'll feed them too. It won't take long.'

'OK.'

Once inside the igloo with the flashlight, while Tommy fed the dogs, Meg confronted Anik. 'Your mother's OK, Anik. Nuna told me. . .and I suspect that Nuna knows everything that there is to know in the village. You know her?'

'Yes,' the girl whispered, her plump-cheeked face raised for a moment so that she could look at Meg with her coal-black eyes.

'When we get back, some arrangement will be made for you to speak to her by telephone tomorrow morning. Are you all right?' she added gently.

Anik nodded in affirmation, putting a hand up quickly to wipe her face. After Tommy had crawled on hands and knees through the small entrance of the snow house, carrying a bag of food, they ate raven-

ously. There was more of the hot chocolate, laced with
brandy, some bannock, which was a type of bread,
and thin slivers of dried caribou meat which the boy cut
up for them with a very sharp knife. The atmosphere
lightened somewhat as they filled their stomachs. Anik
even managed a shy smile when urged to eat by both
of her companions, when Tommy was not questioning
her in Inuktitut, obviously keen to get a very clear
version of her story.

'Listen! I can hear something.' Meg, who had
removed her hood and woollen hat, lifted a finger for
silence. A faint sound, like the distant buzzing of an
insect, could be heard, getting louder. 'I think it's a
skidoo. Do you suppose it's someone come to look for
us, Tom?'

'Maybe. It sounds like more than one.' As they sat
listening, the sound moving rapidly closer, it became
evident to all of them that there were several vehicles.

'We should go out, Tom, quickly, so that they don't
miss us.' Meg made a movement to crawl out, while
Anik spoke rapidly to Tommy in her own language,
her face frightened.

'You wait here,' Tom suggested. 'I will see who it
is. They will see the remains of our fire near the sentinel. Anik is frightened that someone might be angry
with her. I do not think so.'

'It's OK, Anik,' Meg reassured the girl soothingly
when Tommy had gone. 'We're going to take care
of you.'

All at once, it seemed, the area around the igloo was
vibrant with noise from the engines of snowmobiles,
mingled with the sound of jubilantly barking dogs and
shouting voices of men. While Meg thrust the remains
of their meal back into the bag, Anik sat immobile.
Perhaps she had benefited from her brief sojourn away
from other people; perhaps she had found a measure

of peace from her problems, even if she had not exactly enjoyed the solitude. Now it was over.

'Your father's here, Anik.' Tommy's head and shoulders appeared. 'No one is angry with you. . .they are very, very happy. You can come out now. And, Meg, one of the doctors from the medical station is here. . . Dr Russell.'

Wordlessly Anik crawled out, followed by Meg. All was confusion outside. There were four skidoos with their engines idling, their brilliant headlights lighting up the area and the small igloo, which looked now pathetically simple. Dogs barked, people talked, shouted, laughed and cried. While Meg stood looking around her in a daze, Anik was hugged by her father and several other people. Each skidoo had brought two men.

A man, taller and heavier then the others, detached himself from the group and came over to her. 'Craig? Oh, Craig. . .I'm so glad it's you. . . We weren't looking forward to the journey back by ourselves, although no one would admit it,' Meg blurted out at the sight of him. 'We found her. . .we actually found her! Isn't that wonderful!'

If she had thought he would sweep her into his arms with abject relief and, perhaps, declarations of undying love. . .not far from the truth. . .the reality was disappointing. 'What the hell possessed you to come out here with that kid? Are you off your rocker?' His voice grated rudely, rough with anger.

For a few moments she groped for words, her eyes opening wide with shock. This was the first time she had seen him really angry, crudely human. He was like a stranger. 'He's fifteen,' she stated flatly. 'I trusted him. He's very experienced.'

'Gee! All of fifteen!' It was evident that he wanted to pick a fight, his voice sarcastic. 'How much experience do you think a fifteen-year-old can have? Answer me that! And there's a very thin line between trust and naïveté; you were being pretty naïve in coming out here. . .and not very intelligent.' Under cover of the general hubbub, he had raised his voice so that he was practically shouting, his eyes blazing down into hers. How could she have wished, a short while ago, that he would turn up? She had actually missed him!

'I was asked to help. Bonnie Mae and Nuna, as well as the RCMP, knew where we were. . .as you know. We found the girl. Doesn't that mean anything to you?'

'It's great. But you put yourself in danger by doing so. . .and the boy as well. You're here to staff the medical station, not perform heroics. How do you think I felt when I found out you had taken off with a boy?'

'Angry, evidently.'

'You're damn right I was angry! You've been here all of a month and you do something monumentally stupid. I had expected that you, a professional person, would have more sense. Perhaps my original assessment of you was correct, when I first saw you with your arm around that punky little orthopaedic resident. A little on the flighty side, eh, Meg Langham? Someone who acts first and thinks after?'

'Flighty? That's the last thing I am!' she spluttered. 'Anyway, I didn't have my arm around him, he had his arm around me! There is a difference.' She said the first thing that came into her head, hard-pressed to defend herself.

Their breath was like clouds of steam between them in the furious verbal exchange. She faced him, gloved hands clenched, speaking through lips that were stiff with cold and suppressed emotion. Any minute now she would bawl her eyes out if she wasn't careful. So much for dreams and illusion. She remembered

Richard Becker with a sudden longing.

'What has that got to do with the here and now?' she
demanded. 'More importantly, you're not my boss. . .
we're not on duty. . .so just stay away from me and
keep your mouth shut!'

'I've no intention of keeping my mouth shut. Errors
of judgement can be fatal——'

'What's more,' she interrupted him, 'I spent six
months in Jasper Creek, on my own, with no Craig
Russell to tell me what to do or not to do. I know
when to take a calculated risk. And since this seems
to be truth-saying time, you should know that I don't
trust you. . .don't trust you one inch!' Pulling her hood
back over her head to hide the threatened loss of com-
posure, she marched the short distance to the sled,
where she began to untie ropes at a furious pace, to
reposition the remaining boxes for their departure. Her
lips were trembling so much that she had to press them
together in case someone should notice.

Dazedly she accepted the repeated congratulations
and thanks of the men, the repeated handshakes as
the party prepared to depart. . .from all except Craig
Russell. She explained, in a barely audible voice, that
it was Tommy really. . .she hadn't done much. They
insisted that she was a heroine.

It was agreed that she and Anik should bundle up
together under the skin rugs on the wooden sled, which
Tommy would drive again. One skidoo would go
directly in front of them, one directly behind, and the
other two at the sides. In this way they would have
plenty of light, would not have to worry about
obstacles, and so could travel very quickly.

One of the men had a two-way radio, into which he
spoke rapidly in Inuktitut. The whole of Chalmers Bay,
it seemed, knew they were coming back, would be out
to greet them. She and Tommy were little short of

heroes. What would they think if they knew that the heart of the nurse was heavy, that under cover of her voluminous hood warm tears ran down her cheeks?

CHAPTER NINE

WHEN the lights of Chalmers Bay once again became visible as tiny dots in the distance, it also became obvious that a flotilla of vehicles was coming out over the tundra to meet them. Lights weaved and danced like fireflies, low to the ground, recognisable as the headlamps of skidoos. Evidently they were going to make a triumphant entry, the return of the prodigal daughter. Meg half sat, half lay on the speeding *qamutik*, with an arm around Anik, who lay beside her. Cold wind whipped the fur on their hoods.

As Meg held the girl, she felt emotionally warmed by this evidence of the whole community pulling together to save one of their own, glad that she could be a part of it, in spite of Craig's condemnation of her action. He was somewhere in the group, a passenger on one of the vehicles; she did not know which one. She kept her line of vision resolutely ahead.

'Whoa!' Tommy yelled, trying to make his voice heard above the din of the engines when they had at last reached the open area in front of the village church. To help him, there was a general chorus of 'Whoa!' all around them from the waiting villagers.

Everything happened quickly then. People surrounded them, pressing in close as they got up from the *qamutik*. The Anglican priest, distinguishable by a white sash round his shoulders, thrown over his heavy outdoor clothing, was at the forefront of the crowd. It occurred to Meg then, confusedly, that the rescue would have great spiritual significance for the local people. Living in this harsh environment, where a dis-

respect for the power of nature could lead to a quick
death, made such a rescue seem like a benign act of
God, who had interceded on their behalf. Meg stood
beside the girl, holding her arm, while the crowd
pressed round them, so that they and the dog team
were in the centre of a tight circle. No one made a
move to touch or speak to Anik.

Then a very extraordinary thing happened. As
though with one voice, the crowd began to sing. No
one had given a signal. Spontaneously the sound lifted
and swelled in the night air. It was a song of praise
and gratitude, moving like a wave over the assembled
people to unite them and soothe their fear. The words
were in Inuktitut; the tune was familiar.

As Meg, incredulously, recognised the tune of a
familiar hymn, 'Now Thank We All Our God', she
also realised that she was crying, choked with emotion,
as were many people around her. Missionaries had
been in this land during the last century and before,
bringing their religion to these people, who had incor-
porated it into their own ancient beliefs. What she was
now witnessing was the legacy of their work. The old
belief of these people was that man was very much a
part of nature, not above it.

Gasping sobs came from Meg's throat, the sound of
them lost in the surrounding, all-encompassing verbal
music; they were a letting go of the tension that had
been building up, which included an acknowledgement
of her disappointment at Craig's ugly words to her.

Only after the singing had ended did the priest come
forward to clasp Anik in a hug. Over the top of her
head he said a short prayer of thanks as the people
fell silent. Then the jubilation erupted, as though the
first consideration had been accomplished. Anik's
father hugged and kissed her again, then shook Meg's
hand while she sobbed unashamedly. As though this

was a signal, other family members came forward to welcome the girl, all weeping, and to shake hands with Meg and Tommy. Bemused, feeling that she was there somehow under false pretences, Meg would have liked to move to the back of the crowd unnoticed so that Tommy could receive the congratulations that he deserved. Yet she would not have wanted to miss this outpouring of affection and solidarity for anything.

Someone lit candles on the church steps, under the porch where they were sheltered from the wind. Anik was led forward to light a candle, together with a general surge of the crowd. Meg hung back by the sled, noticing that Tommy was lifting up the snow-anchors, preparing to move the team. The dogs, obviously exhausted, would be hungry.

'Do you need any help, Tommy?' she offered.

'No, thank you, Meg. You must take care of yourself now, get warmed up. Thank you for coming with me. Anik will be all right now. Tomorrow there will be a ceremony of thanks, to which you must come.'

Making her way to the back of the crowd, on legs that felt tremulous with fatigue, Meg checked her wristwatch to find that it was half-past two in the morning. As she trudged towards the parked skidoo, her arm was suddenly taken from behind and she was jerked to a halt. 'Meg, wait!' Craig's face, serious and taut, regarded her from the depths of his enveloping hood. 'Where are you heading now? I'm not letting you out of my sight, in case you do something equally stupid.'

If she had not been wearing thick gauntlets, if he had not been so well-padded in turn, she might have slapped his face. The urge to do so, evidenced by a tingling in her right arm, was strong. 'Getting the skidoo,' she said in a tight, controlled voice. 'To go back.'

'Take me with you,' he said, walking along beside

her, large and dominating. 'Let me drive; you must be exhausted.'

Meg said nothing. Yes, she was exhausted. It was something of a relief to sit behind Craig, sheltered by him, as they returned to the medical station in a sedate manner. They were silent as he switched off the engine after their arrival, the memory of his rude words heavy between them.

A wave of warm air, like an enveloping balm, met them as they went through the door to the interior of the clinic. All was silent and dark. 'I want to talk to you, Meg,' Craig said, switching on a light. He looked much as he had when she had first met him, unsmiling, assessing her with shrewd eyes.

'If you're going to give me a lecture, you can save your breath,' she said wearily, aware that in this light he could see her swollen eyelids, the marks of tears on her face. 'Because I don't want to hear it. I'm quite aware of the risk I took.'

His expression changed as he saw the evidence of her distress. 'Actually, I'm going to apologise for being so boorish out there. I was rude, somewhat heavy-handed. Put it down to my anxiety about you. When I went to the RCMP to find out what was going on, then discovered that you had gone out on the search. . .and with a boy. . .I thought you must be crazy. It wouldn't look good if you, a nurse from the medical station, came a cropper after such a short time up here.'

'You're worried that you might somehow be blamed?' she said slowly.

'Not exactly. I just feel that I have a certain responsibility for you because I've been up here in this sort of territory before. Paternalistic though that may sound, it's none the less true.' He pushed back his hood and removed the woollen hat that he wore underneath, running a hand impatiently through his hair.

'I do appreciate your concern. But a self-appointed protector? When you don't really give a damn about me as a person?' she queried drily, then said challengingly, 'I don't think that's part of your mandate up here.'

'When I see a breach, I like to fill it.' The gleam in his eyes told her that he had taken her point, had chosen not to comment.

Watching him, Meg moved her tongue over dry lips that felt sore and chapped, feeling the old familiar effects of his attraction overriding the sobering anger that had simmered within her since his abrasive appearance on the scene. He seemed to take it for granted that he would be in charge of anything and everything.

'I need a hot drink,' she mumbled, turning away. 'Perhaps you wouldn't mind telling Nuna that Anik's safe. She would want to know.'

'I'll make you a hot drink over in the annexe while you get under the shower. You go ahead; I'll talk to Nuna.'

'Um. . .thanks,' she said ungraciously, not having the strength to argue. She felt so stiff with cold that she could easily have wept again. Now that she was back from the adventure she was aware that she felt cold right through to the core of her body, with a deep internal shivering making itself felt. It frightened her suddenly. Craig was right, of course; she had taken risks. She could develop pneumonia, for one thing.

Under the shower she turned on the cascade of water over her body, as hot as she could tolerate it. When she emerged later, suitably and warmly covered by her night attire, she found Craig sitting at the bottom of her bed and a tray with a mug on it on her tiny dressing-table. Feeling self-conscious, she dumped her clothes on a chair, then rummaged in a drawer for wool socks and a cardigan.

'I'm determined to stay warm,' she said by way of explanation, not looking at him as she hastily pulled on the socks, then the loose cardigan over her robe. Without more ado, she clambered into the bed, propped herself up on the pile of pillows, with the blankets and duvet up to her chin.

'Ah, that's better,' she said blissfully, closing her eyes. 'This is sheer heaven.' Her flippant tone belied her acute awareness of him. 'All I need now is that drink. . .very hot.'

'Coming right up,' he said. 'It's hot milk, with honey and brandy.' There was a reluctant amusement in his voice, so that she opened her eyes a slit to observe him. 'I thought you were going to put on a scarf and gloves as well.'

'I'll do that when you've gone,' she joked. 'Plus the hat and the nose-cosy.'

He walked over to hand her the drink as she reluctantly sat up. 'I wasn't necessarily planning on going,' he said.

Nonplussed, already flushed and hot from the shower, Meg felt the heat take on a new quality. 'What is that supposed to mean?' she asked, while keeping her lowered gaze concentrated on the mug as she sipped from it.

The bed sagged as he sat down on the side of it, close to her. 'Perhaps you would rather not be alone,' he said evenly, meeting her enquiring eyes levelly. 'That was quite an ordeal out there.'

Quite unable to think of anything to say, Meg stared at him, her green eyes wide. Even though they had once been lovers she felt, if anything, more unsure of how to respond now than she had then. Since that time she had often fantasised about how she would

behave in just such a situation as this, had imagined
her own sophisticated, glib responses. Now all sophisti-
cation left her.

'I don't mean what you probably think I mean,' he
said evenly. 'I would just sit in the room with you for
a while, until you're asleep.'

'Thanks. . .that's kind of you. I'll be all right,
I think.'

Embarrassed by her own presumption, she was both
relieved and dismayed when he got up.

'I'll leave my door open, and yours,' he said.
'Call me if there's anything you need. After the
chill you've had, you could possibly develop a high
temperature.'

She was in a high, wide, dark tunnel which had glisten-
ing, strangely luminescent sides that were running with
water. As she walked, water dripped on to her head;
there were stalagmites and stalactites through which
she had to pass; they grew closer together as she
moved, until she found that she had to push her way
through them. With each step her feet became heavier.
Then, wanting to turn back, she found that she was
lost; the tunnel had disappeared in the forest of wet,
dripping columns. Frantically turning this way and that,
her body strangely heavy, her feet dragging, she
searched for the way she had come. . .and could not
find it.

'Craig, Craig. . .Craig!'

Meg sat bolt upright, for a few seconds experiencing
a sense of intense fear, not knowing where she was.
Conscious then of beads of perspiration covering her
face, her heart pounding, she recognised the dim outline of the furniture in her room, visible in a faint light
that penetrated from the electric light outside, near
the annexe entrance. She had had an awful dream,

more like a nightmare. The lighted digits on her bed-side clock read five forty-five.

Feeling a great thirst, she got swiftly out of bed, to be overcome for a few seconds by a wave of faintness. As she steadied herself against the edge of the bed, it did not take her long to realise that, judging by the slight fever that she undoubtedly had, the headache, the sweating, she had caught a cold, or worse. Wrapping herself in the duvet from the bed, she padded out to the kitchen and put on the light. There were cartons of orange juice there. Thirstily she drank a glass of the juice and poured herself another.

'Meg, are you all right? I heard you call my name.'

'Oh. . .' She had not heard him coming. Craig stood in the doorway, wearing a thick blue towelling dressing-gown. 'I'm sorry if I woke you; I must have called out in my sleep. I had the most awful dream. . .about being lost in a cave, or something.' She found that she felt too unwell to be shy of the fact that she looked somewhat bizarre, still wearing the wool socks and cardigan over her crumpled robe, the whole lot wrapped in a duvet, her hair a mass of tangled curls. 'Predictably, I'm not feeling too good at the moment. Thank God tomorrow's a day off. With any luck I'll be OK by Monday.' As he watched she drank another glass of juice.

'Come and sit on the sofa,' he offered. 'I'll take your temperature. I still have one of those old-fashioned thermometers somewhere.' He didn't quite say 'I told you so', yet there was a certain inflexion in his voice, a professional censure.

'Thanks. I am feeling a little dizzy.' She suffered him to make her comfortable on the sofa, cover her with the duvet, then while he was absent looking for the thermometer she cursed her luck. Somehow she had to nip this thing in the bud so that she was well enough for work on Monday. There was simply no leeway for any of the staff to get sick in this place.

'Here, under the tongue.' Obediently she opened her mouth to receive the thermometer when Craig sat down heavily beside her. 'I want to listen to your chest as well.'

She kept her eyes lowered as he moved the cool tip of the stethoscope over her bare chest, holding her breath as his fingers touched her breasts, then over her back, carefully listening to the air moving in and out of her lungs, listening for any tell-tale changes that would indicate she had pneumonia.

'Your lungs are more or less clear at the moment,' he said, standing up to put the stethoscope on the table, to take the thermometer from her mouth. 'The temperature's up a bit, but not enough to worry about. I want to give you some tablets to lower the temperature, and a decongestant. If you stay in bed today, rest, sleep, maybe you'll be OK.'

'I'm awfully sorry, Craig, to be such a nuisance. You've been so. . .so sweet. Quite a change. . .but you have. I really didn't mean to wake you.' Meg found her eyes straying to his bare chest between the lapels of his dressing-gown.

'Don't be so bloody English,' he said without rancour, his tone even. 'Just relax. I'll get the tablets. I have some ointment too that might help. It's an old-fashioned remedy, but effective. I don't like giving antibiotics until I know what you've got.'

As she swallowed the tablets he waited for her patiently. 'Turn over, under the duvet,' he said. 'That should protect your modesty. You'll have to take off that woollen jacket.'

Meg discarded a few garments and arranged herself face down on the sofa under the duvet. 'I have to admit that my chest is feeling just a little tight.'

'Sure it is,' he said.

As she felt him ease the soft material of her night-dress up over her back to form a roll at the top of her shoulders, as she again felt his touch on her skin, she knew that this was a mistake. But there was nothing she wanted to do about it. The ointment gave off a pungent scent of pine and eucalyptus; it was cool at first as he dotted it over the skin of her back, then became warm as he smoothed his hands firmly, sensuously over her body, moving up slowly from her waist to her shoulders. The vapour made her eyes water and began to clear her nostrils.

'Mmm, that's nice. . .I like the scent,' she murmured, feeling her whole body come alive under his touch, warmed to a hyper-awareness of him as he sat on the edge of the sofa beside her. Her heavy eyelids drooped shut. It was all she could do not to squirm with pleasure, to turn over and offer herself to him unreservedly, in spite of feeling ill.

'It's nice for me too,' he said softly, so that she was not sure she had heard him.

The slight irritant effect of the ingredients of the ointment worked on her skin to make it feel hot, soothed. For a long time he continued to smooth his hands over her, until she was on the verge of a blissful sleep. Then he paused and she felt his lips on the back of her neck where her hair had parted. Scarcely daring to breathe, she heard him sigh and stand up.

'Get back to bed, Meg,' he said. 'I'll stay with you this time until you're asleep.'

As she moved languidly back to her bed she was intensely aware of the desire, unguarded, that was there between them, as it had been on that hot night when they had made love in Gresham, that breezy, stormy night, when the scent of summer flowers had filled his house. . .

This time he did not touch her, but lay beside her silently until the decongestant began to have an effect and she felt sleep taking over. Although she would not have admitted it to him, she was grateful for his presence. She remembered then, in another life, how he had taught her what sexual pleasure meant. . .she thought of the woman about whom she knew so little, who came between them constantly—the woman who had been Rob's mother, the woman Craig had loved. . .

CHAPTER TEN

A MURMUR of voices woke Meg late in the day on Sunday; one was a woman's twangy tones, and another one was Rob's. She stirred and stretched in the warm bed, feeling considerably better in health.

Bonnie Mae, on learning of her illness, had practically ordered her to take Monday off, and the Tuesday if necessary. Apparently, according to Bonnie, she was a heroine in Chalmers Bay following the rescue of Anik. There had indeed been a ceremony of thanksgiving at the church, which she had missed that morning. As for Anik herself, she appeared to be in good health and had spoken to her mother in Edmonton by telephone.

'What's wrong with you?' a voice enquired from the doorway. Rob stood there looking at her enquiringly.

'Just a cold, I think.' She smiled at him. 'How are you?'

'OK,' he said a little sombrely.

'Rob!' The woman's voice called him out, then she appeared herself. 'That kid,' she said with exasperation. 'As much as I adore him, he gets a bit much at times. Sorry he busted in here without being asked. Hi, I'm Gail Adamson.'

'Hello,' Meg murmured. 'I don't mind him being here.'

Gail had a slightly weathered 'outdoor' face, with the remains of an old tan, and fine lines radiating from her eyes when she smiled. Not a *femme fatale* at all, Meg realised, just ordinarily attractive.

'Craig's a saint, taking on that kid,' Gail went on,

not seeming to have heard Meg's soft rejoinder. 'He could have got out of it if he'd tried. How you feeling?'

'A lot better, thanks.'

Craig appeared behind Gail, and Meg had the impression that he had heard her remarks. What exactly did she mean—'he could have got out of it'?

'Ready to leave, Gail?' he said.

'Sure.' After a swift, assessing glance from one to the other, Gail left the room and Craig turned his attention to Meg.

'OK?' he asked softly, concerned, his old reserve back, with only a hint of something in his expression to indicate that he was moved by her tumbled, very feminine appearance. 'Rob's staying here for the evening so that Gail can go out. I'll keep him quiet so that he doesn't disturb you.'

'Oh, please don't,' she protested. 'I could use a little childish chatter in the background. I'm much better.'

It was sheer heaven to have the Monday off. She spent most of the day in bed, getting up for a shower in the late afternoon, before dressing and making herself tea and a snack. The incipient cold, the tightness in her chest, had gone. The telephone rang as she was drinking her tea. It was Dan, inviting himself over to talk about work.

'Come on over, Dan,' she invited. 'You can have some tea.'

It was so easy to be relaxed with Dan, Meg reflected when she saw him; he seemed so ordinary and uncomplicated, as far as anyone was ever ordinary.

'Well, Meg,' he said, ensconced in a chair with a mug of tea in his hand, having congratulated her on being a heroine in Chalmers Bay, 'Anik will be coming to see us some time today. The priest telephoned earlier; he's been talking to her and her family and he's concluded that we should discuss her mother's illness with her, then give her counselling on a daily basis, at least until her mother comes back, which may be next week. She's spoken to her mother twice now by telephone, so at least she's reassured that her mother's alive.'

'That's wonderful!'

'I know you're off sick, but I think you should be one of the people to talk to her. I would like to be in on it as well. I guess that the rest of her family didn't explain things to her adequately before her mother went away. Bonnie Mae said that somehow an explanation to the girl got overlooked. It just proves, I guess, that you shouldn't assume certain things will get done. . .best to do them yourself. I thought we could do it over here this time; it's more relaxed here.'

'Is she coming of her own free will,' Meg asked, thinking that perhaps the girl had been coerced into accepting counselling, 'or was she persuaded by the priest?'

'Mostly the latter, I think. Probably she wouldn't take the initiative herself. . .she's too young and unsophisticated. Neither would her family, I suspect, ask for help. So there you are! It's up to us.'

'Yes, I agree.'

'We can discuss her mother's condition, accentuate the positive aspects of it, now that she's had the hysterectomy and won't be getting any more heavy bleeding.'

'Perhaps we could get Anik involved in her mother's care and treatment, as the mother's a diabetic—let her feel that she's not just helpless,' Meg said, warming to the possibilities.

'Good idea,' Dan agreed, getting up. 'Then once we've got Anik's co-operation maybe she'll talk more about herself and her own worries.'

'Mmm. I have to confess that I haven't done any

actual counselling before, as such, although it's part
and parcel of our job all the time, of course, in short,
sharp doses.'

'I'm sure you'll be great.' Dan grinned at her. 'Well,
I must go. I'll give you a call when she's here, eh?'

'Yes,' she agreed. 'I won't be going anywhere.
Thanks, Dan.'

In the moments of peaceful silence that followed his
departure, Meg poured herself more tea and contemplated all that had happened in the short time that she
had been in Chalmers Bay. Heavy footsteps on the
wooden floor of the covered way caught her attention
and she looked expectantly at the door, aware of a
sudden increase in her heart-rate as she waited.

'Hi. . .' Craig came into the room, bringing with him
a momentary blast of cool air, making her shiver. 'How
are you feeling?'

'A lot better, thanks. I'm planning to go to work
tomorrow,' she answered. 'In fact, this afternoon I'm
going to help Dan talk to the girl we rescued. I guess
that could be construed as work.'

'There's a lull over there at the moment, so I decided
to take a break,' he said in a businesslike manner,
pouring himself tea. To Meg he looked drawn and
tired. 'Besides, I want to talk to you.' When he sat
down opposite her, fixing her with that shrewd,
assessing look that she knew so well, she was the first
to break eye contact.

'I thought you might,' she confessed quietly. How
could he not, when he had vowed not so long ago that
he wouldn't touch her with a barge pole? What an
awful expression that was.

'I seem to have. . .what shall I say?. . .forgotten
my good intentions last night,' he began, leaning
forward, not taking his eyes off her.

'Don't let it worry you,' she said, with effort, remembering the unnecessarily prolonged time that he had taken to smooth his hands over her receptive body.

'Let's put it down to the fact that you were on the verge of incipient pneumonia, shall we?' he said smoothly.

'Yes. . .let's,' she agreed. They might have been discussing tomorrow's operating list, she thought wildly as she looked at him, trying not to let him see that she would welcome that touch now. He gave little away himself; only a certain tightness in the line of his jaw indicated that he, perhaps, shared her need.

'There's something you should know. . .something that will perhaps help you to grow up,' he said compellingly. 'Because a man and a woman enjoy sex together, it doesn't mean that they have to love each other, or have any intentions of permanence. They do need to like each other, to feel affection, to have a mutual respect, as well as the sexual thing. . . Apart from that, it can be pure, unmitigated pleasure. All my women have understood that.'

'Yes, I know that,' she said. 'Please don't give me a lecture on human relationships. Why. . .why are you saying this to me?'

'I want to know what makes you tick,' he said. 'I'm still trying to figure out why you really left Gresham, when we had something good going for us.'

'I want more,' she forced herself to articulate, 'than a simple physical arrangement. I want love.'

'And you didn't love me!' he said flatly, his lips twisting with a cynical amusement. 'And your puritan soul would not let you enjoy the pleasure. . .I know it was a pleasure for you. Is that it?'

'No!' Meg could hardly get the word out. They seemed to be going round in circles. If he didn't know that she loved him, he must be stupid. . .yet she didn't really think he was. If she admitted it now, as she longed to do, she suspected that he would go back on his word and resume their explosive sexual union. And not only would she get hurt, she would be devastated somewhere down the road. 'I was frightened of getting hurt. . .of being used. Did you. . .did you love me?' It was her turn to be sarcastic now, although her sarcasm was a cover-up. 'I suspect your pride was momentarily hurt, if I may presume so much!'

'Well, Meg Langham, you can be bitchy!' He raised his eyebrows at her, above those coolly assessing eyes that made her weak with an unsatisfied anticipation whenever she looked into them. 'So you were frightened of being hurt! Let's say it was frustrated desire on my part. Men and women are different. . . With men, desire comes first, then sex. . .then love, if it is to come at all,' he said.

'Does it?' she said, keeping her eyes lowered to her hands, clasped tightly in her lap. 'Very convenient.' She forced herself to add, 'With me, it would stop at the sex. . .is that it?'

'I don't kid myself you give a damn about me,' he said, ignoring her question. 'You like the physical thing as much as I do; there's no mistaking that. If you know the score, you shouldn't get hurt.'

'That doesn't necessarily follow.' The bitter, twisted face of Joyce Travers came to her mind, together with that of Joyce's friend Cynthia, both of whom had perhaps loved him from afar, the unattainable Dr Russell. 'You seem to have left a few broken hearts behind you in Gresham,' she somehow found the courage to say, feeling that she now had nothing to lose.

'I doubt that,' he said.

They might have continued sparring for some time, had they not been interrupted. Meg thought she knew what Craig was doing; he was trying to prepare the way for a resumption of their former relationship later.

without giving anything of himself away, while still having a relationship with Gail, the permanent one. . .

When Dan unexpectedly appeared again in the annexe, Meg felt such a flood of relief that she could have hugged him.

'Anik's here now,' he informed her. 'She's come with an aunt.' He looked at them both sharply. 'You're not haranguing the poor girl again, are you, Craig? About going out on the tundra? There's a bit of an atmosphere in here, to say the least. You could cut it with a knife.'

'You're quite right, Dan.' Craig stood up.

'He does tend to bully me, you know,' Meg said as brightly as she could, jumping to her feet. 'But I can handle him. I'm ready when you are, Dan. Just come on over with Anik.'

'Great! Can you take care of things, Craig, while I'm over here?'

'Sure.'

For the next hour Dan and Meg talked to and listened to the girl, while her aunt remained in the waiting-room. It all came out then, her fears and worries. The sixteen-year-old boy, Tarsis, whom Anik regarded as her boyfriend—although she conceded that he might not exactly think of her as his girlfriend in the accepted sense—had gone down south to school, where he would be for the next two years. He was a bright boy, she explained hesitantly, who hoped to get into a university down there when he was eighteen. She talked about her own option of possibly going there herself in the future, expressed her hopes and conflicting fears about leaving her home and family, all that was familiar to her, to go hundreds of miles to an alien culture.

Meg pointed out that Anik had quite a long time in which to think about this matter, that she was under

no obligation to go, and that as she matured the solution would become clear to her. Tarsis would be back
for the summer holiday, after all. They talked about
her mother's illness, about how she could help later.

By the time the session was at an end, Anik seemed
happier, more at peace with herself. Obviously she was
not used to talking about herself, of her innermost
feelings; it seemed to come as a big surprise that doing
so could bring a profound psychological relief. They
all agreed that they would talk every day; it was an
informal arrangement, so that she would not feel
intimidated, yet very definite, so that she knew she
was committed.

It did not escape Meg during the session that she
could use some of her own advice herself; it was always
so much easier to give advice when you were not emotionally involved yourself. All the old sayings, like not
letting your heart rule your head, were difficult to
dwell on in the heat of the moment. Human relationships, human passions, were fraught with danger.

These thoughts occupied Meg's mind when she again
sat in her own room, trying to write a letter to her
friend, Jen, telling her that she would be interested in
any vacant position. The biblical words 'Physician, heal
thyself' came to her forcefully. . .

CHAPTER ELEVEN

THE remainder of the week proved to be hectic. There was little need for Meg and Craig to be together outside of work. On the Friday evening, when she arrived at the medical station to do a late shift with an in-patient, Bonnie Mae gave her some welcome news.

'By the way, Meg, I've been talking to the hospital in Edmonton about Anik's mother. They've booked her on a flight to come home on Wednesday next week. A nurse from down there will be coming with her. I was wondering if you would like to be the one to give Anik the news?'

'Yes, I'll be happy to be the one to tell her.'

'I am so much wanting my mother back,' Anik said quietly, her girlish, round-cheeked face looking wistful, when Meg told her the news on the Saturday, having taken the skidoo to the girl's house. 'Although she has not really been gone for very long, it seems years to me since I last saw her.'

'Yes. . .I know.' Meg squeezed her hand. 'Someone from the medical station will be at the airstrip to meet her plane. Maybe the school would give you time off to come with us. Shall I see if I can arrange it? Then I'll pick you up from here.'

'Yes, please.' Anik smiled.

Although Meg and Craig were both on call that weekend, he spent quite a lot of time out with Rob, and with him back at the annexe, so that she was seldom alone with him. Meg was becoming very fond of Rob, and he seemed to be attached to her, tending to follow her about, chattering, when he was visiting

155

the annexe. Sometimes she found herself thinking that they were almost like a family. Perhaps, she speculated, Gail thought that too when she was with father and son. Most of the time Meg tried not to think of them with Gail.

It was not until the Sunday evening, when Rob had been taken home, that Meg had a chance to be with Craig, to ask him the question that had been nagging at her for nearly a week.

'What did Gail mean when she made the comment that you could have got out of having Rob?' she asked him point-blank after they had finished a simple supper together, having spent the entire meal plucking up the courage. 'I think you must have loved his mother very much. . .I would like to know the whole story, so that I can understand.'

Craig swallowed the last of the red wine that they had been drinking. They sat on opposite sides of the small dining-table.

'Tell me to mind my own business if you want to,' she blundered on, 'but. . .I would really like to know.'

'OK. . .so be it,' he said, staring at the empty glass, turning it around absently in his fingers, no doubt mellowed by the wine. 'Sonia. . .that's Rob's mother. . . was only seventeen when I met her, at a party. She said she was twenty-two, the same age that I was, and she looked it. She was the child of a very wealthy family. . .lots of money, not much love; she was the classic mixed-up kid.' He looked up, his eyes unsmiling. 'The pregnancy happened very soon after I met her.'

That was a rather odd way of putting it, Meg thought, forcing herself to meet his eyes, not trusting herself to comment.

'Her parents were divorced; they tried to pretend that it wasn't happening. . .the pregnancy, then her illness. She moved in with my mother. Between us, we took care of them both.' There was a cynical harshness in him now as he informed her of the facts.

'Why wouldn't she marry you?' Meg said it softly.

'Is that what you would have done?'

Bravely she said what was on her mind. 'She probably loved you. . .and then there was the baby. . .'

'Don't be naïve, Meg. He was not. . .is not. . .my son. Sonia didn't tell me that, of course. I had a DNA test done to find out whether I was Rob's father—so-called DNA finger-printing. I was curious. I wanted to know exactly where I stood with him.'

'I'm so sorry, Craig. I had no idea.'

'It doesn't matter,' he said brusquely. 'When the test came back, it was just as I suspected. I had never suggested to Sonia that I was suspicious. . .she was so needy. . .then I had a pretty good idea early on what the outcome of her illness would be; she must have known that the kid wasn't mine. There was no point in lumbering her with that. By not marrying me, she kept a kind of honour. . .by not making me publicly responsible for her condition. She needed me desperately to take care of her, so we played a kind of game. . .both pretending that I was the father. . .until I came to almost believe it myself.'

Restlessly he got up to pace the room, talking rapidly as though, having started, he could not stop. 'I loved the boy, like a son, so the fact that he was not mine didn't matter. I simply took him on.'

'And Sonia?' she whispered.

'I didn't love her. . .not in the way you mean.' The look he gave her was cynical as he stopped his pacing to stand near her. 'I guess I loved her like a brother loves his sister, in the end. I elected to take care of her. That is what I did. I made sure to adopt Rob so that her crazy family wouldn't get their hands on him.

Rob will never know that he's not my natural son;
there's no point in telling him, when we've no idea
who his real father is. If Sonia knew, she didn't let
on. No one knows but Gail, and now you. Not even
my mother.'

It was difficult to think of something appropriate to
say, so Meg remained silent. Even when she had
thought that the boy looked nothing like Craig,
she had not suspected that he really might not be
his son.

'If you're thinking of saying how noble it is of me
to take on somebody else's child, forget it!' Craig said
harshly when she simply looked at him. 'I love that
kid more than anyone or anything in the world. I got
the best of the bargain, believe me. I used to be a
cynical bastard, perhaps having seen too much of the
harsh side of life in med school, as well as after.'

'I wasn't going to say that.'

'No? But you do judge me by my reputation, don't
you, Meg? I've seen the expression on your face
sometimes. . .a certain prissiness in the way you speak
to me. Mmm? That awful Dr Russell who had a baby
out of wedlock, who sleeps around. Isn't that right?'
he persisted,

'Partially. Perhaps if you were more open, more
often, you wouldn't be judged in that way. You judge
me too. You've called me "flighty", and some of my
decisions "not very intelligent",' she reminded him,
trying not to sound defensive. 'Anyway. . .thank you
for explaining. I'm sorry if you feel I've invaded your
privacy,' she said quietly, her steady voice belying the
emotion that the explanation had aroused. 'Would you
like more coffee? Then I really have to go over to the
clinic to check on a few things for tomorrow.'

He laughed out loud then, a mirth that she knew
was at her expense. 'Back to normal now, is it, Meg?

Yes, why not play the hand-maiden role and give me a cup of coffee? Tame the awful Dr Russell with the accoutrements of domesticity!'

'I don't know what you mean. You can do it yourself if you want to,' she said stiffly, going quickly to the kitchen to boil more water.

'Come off it!' he said. 'I'm well aware of the rumours about me. In fact, I took a certain pleasure. . .you might say perverted. . .in deliberately not denying them. Let people think what the hell they like.'

He came to lounge against the doorpost, to watch her, his presence overwhelming the small room; there was a certain remoteness about him, a withdrawal. In spite of what he had said about his love for the boy, he had been badly duped by a woman, not least by his own sense of compassion. Meg's feelings for him were taking new, complicated turns. As he took the proffered mug of coffee from her, his hand covered hers for a second, deliberately, and he laughed softly when she withdrew quickly.

With the imprint of his touch on her, she walked stiffly to her room without looking back. Carefully she locked the door behind her, then did the same when she was in the bathroom. She held a towel against her face to soak up her tears, biting on the soft material to muffle the sound of her crying. There seemed to be little trust left in him and all his love seemed to be directed towards the small boy who had no mother and no known father. It seemed to her then that the message from him had been very clear.

Wednesday proved to be hectic. It was a day of booked day-surgery cases, as well as a day of minor accidents. Meg had been warned that as the weather got steadily warmer there would be more accidents as the local people increased their outdoor activities and the

children and teenagers went a little mad with joy after
the incarceration of winter.

Meg was hard-pressed to get to the airstrip on time
to meet the Edmonton flight. As she and Anik
approached the strip in the medical station's pick-up
truck they saw the jet coming in to land, like a great
majestic silver bird.

'Oh. . .Mama, Mama,' Anik whispered from her
seat beside Meg, in a fever of longing and impatience.

'Don't worry, we'll be there in plenty of time,' Meg
assured her.

They watched from a window in the terminal building while the steps for the passengers were put in
position, then the door of the aircraft opened. Immediately passengers came out, descending the steps.

'She's not there,' Anik said in agony, turning tor-
tured, frightened eyes to Meg.

'I expect she'll get off last,' Meg said, trying not to
share the girl's fear that something might have happened at the last minute to prevent her mother from
coming. As they waited, Greg Farley turned up with
Anik's father.

'Hi there, Meg,' Greg greeted her. 'I'm here to take
the family home. We're going to put up the nurse from
Edmonton at the RCMP headquarters.'

'OK,' she answered him, marvelling at the efficiency
of the community co-ordination and the local grapevine
of communication. Little was left to chance. 'Anik's
worried that her mother might not be on the plane.'

'I haven't heard anything to suggest that,' Greg said.

'Here she comes!' Anik's father said, standing
beside them.

They could now see that a wheelchair was being
lifted out of the aircraft door, with two men at the top
end and two at the bottom doing the lifting. The figure
in the wheelchair was muffled up in blankets. Slowly

the chair was lifted step by step down to the frozen snow, then the men carried it to the terminal.

'Oh, Mama, Mama!' Anik said again, shifting from one foot to the other. She had begun to cry softly with relief, yet Meg could sense that she was also crying with fear lest her mother should be radically changed in some way. They all moved over to be near the door where the mother would come in.

As the wheelchair was pushed through the double doors, the woman in it emerged from her cocoon of coverings to free her head and arms. Meg saw a thin woman with short, glossy black hair, middle-aged. She looked pale and tired as anyone would after a long journey, yet to Meg she did not appear ill; her eyes were alert and shining, her face alive with anticipation. When she saw Anik she held out her arms and called something that was unintelligible to Meg. The girl ran forward, practically falling into her mother's lap as they embraced, holding on to each other as though they would never let go. That was the first time that Anik's mother had ever been away from Chalmers Bay. Meg and the others hung back until mother and daughter, both in tears, were ready to move forward.

'Are you the nurse at the medical station here?' A woman had detached herself from a small clutch of people around the door, to approach Meg.

'Yes. I brought the daughter here.'

'I'm the nurse from the Edmonton hospital.' They introduced themselves. 'I'll give you the medical chart that I've brought with me, shall I? I'm booked on a flight out tomorrow, so I've got time to come up to the medical station a little later on to talk to the doctor there about Mrs Pangnark. She's fine now, actually. . . sure better than when she arrived in Edmonton.'

A change had certainly come over Anik, who was chattering and laughing, holding on to her mother's

hand tightly. Meg said goodbye to her as she helped
her and her mother into Greg Farley's truck for the
ride to their home. Everyone was smiling. The nurse
and Anik's father came with Meg. After she had
deposited the nurse at the RCMP headquarters, with
a promise to see her later at the medical station, she
returned to the clinic for a much needed short tea-
break before helping Bonnie Mae and Nuna with the
day-surgery patients in the recovery-room. There
had been no time, she reflected briefly, to dwell on
her own private life; she had been truly taken out
of herself.

Adele James came the next day to be given the
final word on her breast lump, the pathologist's report
having arrived. As they had suspected, the diagnosis
was that of fibro-adenoma, a non-malignant tumour.

'It's great not to have any in-patients, eh?' Bonnie
Mae commented a little later, in between bites of a
sandwich, as the two nurses and Nuna took a welcome
tea-break in the clinic area, while the two doctors were
having their tea over in the annexe.

'Better not speak too soon,' Nuna commented.
'Maybe you put a jinx on us by saying that. Maybe
this is the lull before the storm.'

'In that case,' Bonnie Mae said, helping herself to
a chocolate doughnut, 'I'm going to make sure that
I keep my blood-sugar level good and high. Have a
doughnut, Meg. You never know when you can get to
eat again in this place! Actually, I'm getting a bit of
a cold, and they do say feed a cold, starve a fever.'

'Since when did you need an excuse to eat, Bonnie?'
Nuna said.

They heard a pick-up truck come up to park outside,
then the door of the clinic open a few minutes later.
Bonnie Mae hastily stuffed the remains of her doughnut in her mouth and licked the chocolate off her

fingers. 'I'll go; you finish eating,' she mumbled. 'Maybe I should have kept my big mouth shut.'

When she returned about ten minutes later she looked very serious, her stethoscope swinging from her hand. 'Meg, would you take a look at this guy who's just come in? His name's Isaac Tataniq, sixty-two years old, works at the hydroelectric plant. . .he's a smoker, too. If he's got what I think he's got, we have something serious on out hands. Before I call the docs over I want to have a good idea of what to tell them. He's got a rapid pulse, blood-pressure too low, and abdominal pain. Tell me what you think, Meg, before I tell you what I think.'

'OK.'

'Take your stethoscope, run it over his abdomen as well as his chest. Nuna, better get the OR ready stat! You know what to do? Major abdominal!'

'OK, Bonnie.' Nuna got to her feet quickly. 'So you did jinx us after all!'

'Looks like it, don't it?'

In the cubicle that Bonnie Mae indicated, Meg saw a somewhat overweight Inuit man lying on the examination table. There were beads of sweat on his upper lip and forehead, his skin unnaturally pale. Without wasting any time on greetings, Meg put her stethoscope to his chest, where she could here a rapid beating, fainter than it should be. When she moved the stethoscope to his abdomen, where she judged the big artery, the aorta, to be, she could hear an unusual sound, like a faint, distant roaring. His skin, when she placed a hand on his arm, was clammy and cool. Bonnie Mae had already charted the blood-pressure.

Outside the cubicle the other nurse took her arm and led her out of earshot of the patient and his wife. 'What's the verdict?'

'Well. . .it could be a leaking abdominal aneurysm,

I think. Something is definitely bleeding,' she
ventured.

'I agree. That thing could blow any time, in my
opinion. Look, I'm going to take him straight to the
OR, explain the score to him, get a couple of IVs
going, get a stomach tube down. What's the bet that
he had a couple of pizzas for lunch, eh?' She gave a
wry grin. 'Call the docs, tell them to get over here
stat. Then get out every bag of blood and plasma we've
got. OK?'

While Bonnie Mae hurried off to get a stretcher,
Meg ran back to the office to snatch up the internal
telephone, her mind buzzing with all the preparations
that she would have to make before they were ready
to operate. Time was of the essence. As Bonnie had
said, if that aneurysm ruptured, if it was indeed a
weakening and ballooning out of the aorta that she had
heard through the stethoscope, the man could bleed to
death in a matter of minutes. It was clear that it was
already leaking blood.

Craig answered the telephone over in the annexe
and Meg heard her own voice tremble a little. 'Craig,
we have a man over here with a possible dissecting
abdominal aneurysm. We're getting the OR ready.
Could you both come right away?'

'Sure. . .we're on our way. How much blood have
we got on hand?'

'At least ten units, plus the fresh-frozen plasma.
There was a new shipment in this morning.'

Next she ran to the small lab area to get five units
of blood out of the refrigerating unit and some plasma
out of the ice-box. The patient was already in the OR,
with one IV running.

'I'll scrub for this, Meg, if you don't mind being the
circulating nurse. Nuna's not trained to be in the OR
while we're operating,' Bonnie Mae called to her when

she appeared. 'Can you check that we've got plenty of heparin and protamine sulphate, and get it out?'

'OK.' With her brain cleared of all extraneous considerations, Meg went about her business swiftly and efficiently, going through the drawers of the anaesthetic cart for the drugs.

'What about artery graft material?' she said tersely to Bonnie Mae. 'Is there any kept here?'

'Yeah, we have some Dacron grafts. . .over in that cupboard with the arterial catheters; get some of those out too, Meg!'

Bonnie Mae was already scrubbing at the sinks outside the room when the two doctors arrived. While Craig went straight to the patient to examine him, to clinch the diagnosis, Dan began to prepare for the anaesthetic. 'If you'll take some blood for the cross-match, Craig,' Dan said, 'I'll set it up before we make a start.'

'Sure. I'll put in the urinary catheter too. Can you help me with that, Meg? I'll do the operation, Dan will give the anaesthetic.'

For the next few minutes they all made haste in a calm, highly organised manner. Bonnie Mae had already inserted a stomach tube, through which the remains of any meal could be aspirated. Mr Tataniq lay passively, obviously apprehensive but resigned, appearing to have faith in the professionals around him. As Craig and Dan examined him, Craig explained what they would have to do. Both doctors confirmed the diagnosis. Meg's respect for Bonnie Mae increased.

'Tie me up, Meg, please.' Having come in from the scrub sinks, Bonnie Mae had put on her sterile gown and was waiting patiently for Meg to secure the ties at the back of the gown.

It took three of them to ease Mr Tataniq on to the operating table, to position him properly, with the bags of IV fluids on poles at either side of the table. Dan prepared to start the anaesthetic.

Craig drew Meg aside, with an arm casually around her shoulders. 'We shouldn't be doing this here, as I'm sure you realise. But we don't have any choice,' he murmured to her. 'Just stay very prepared, honey. . . Get out every damn thing you think we might need; have it ready. Keep close tabs on the amount of blood loss. If it's all relatively straightforward, we should be OK. But we could get into trouble after, with bleeding or clots.'

'How many of these have you done before?' She raised her eyebrows enquiringly at him, very aware of the comforting warmth from his hand through the cotton of her uniform.

'As a matter of fact, I do occasionally assist Dr Rutter, the vascular guy at Gresham. You never know when anything like that is going to come in handy! You doubting me or something?' His eyes were smiling, albeit with a rueful glint in them.

'No, no. Just curious,' she protested innocently.

'Sure! I'm going to get scrubbed now. This is going to be just like the old days. And I've got the best nurse in the place.' With a barely perceptible squeeze to her shoulder, he turned away.

'Ready to count the sponges, Bonnie?' she said.

'Yep.'

Ten minutes later Craig made the incision.

They had been at it for about an hour and a half when the telephone with the outside line rang in the operating-room. Meg—with her gloved hands full of used sponges that she was about to weigh to assess blood loss—pressed the intercom button with her foot, conveniently placed near the floor for that purpose. That would enable her to speak without picking up the receiver, and everyone in the room could hear the amplified voice of the caller.

'Hello, Chalmers Bay medical station,' she said.

'Hi! This is Wayne Keeling of the RCMP,' a loud voice filled the room. 'We've had a call from the coast-guard, Search and Rescue; they need a doctor to go with them to the old Carter Lake gold-mine, right away. They've had a small cave-in near the surface, where no one expected a cave-in; two men are trapped under rubble. That mine's been abandoned temporarily, as you know. . . A few guys from the Black Lake mine were over there bringing out some equipment and got into some sort of trouble. Don't know all the details. Their own paramedics are dealing with some other emergency at the moment. . .the Black Lake guys, that is. . .otherwise they would go.'

The voice was terse, breaking their concentration. For a few seconds there was a horrified silence as they looked at each other, suddenly suspended from the tasks in which they had been engaged.

'Any chance that one of you could come?' Wayne Keeling's voice came again. 'There's a coastguard heli-copter waiting at the airstrip now. We could come and get you.'

The operation on Mr Tataniq had been going well. The diagnosis had indeed been correct, with the certainty that the aneurysm would have ruptured if they had not intervened. They conferred with each other silently.

Bonnie Mae was the first to recover. 'You'll have to go, Meg. There's no way we can spare a doctor right now. As for me, I don't feel too good. . .getting sick, I guess.'

'What was that?' Wayne Keeling queried.

'We could send a nurse,' Dan spoke up. 'We're in the middle of a big operation here; we can't spare a doctor. What injuries do you anticipate?'

'Well, we guess the usual. . .fractures, bleeding, hypothermia, maybe head injuries. There's guys there digging 'em out. A nurse would be fine. Bring your own equipment.'

'Hang on a second, will you, Wayne?' Craig spoke from where he stood beside the operating table. 'We just need to confer with each other.

'Are you willing to go, Meg? Think you can handle it?'

'Yes.' Her mind was already racing ahead, changing tack from the highly controlled milieu of the operating theatre to the more uncertain arena of accident and first aid in the field, in this case the barrens. Even if she didn't think she could handle it, there was no way she could say so.

'We have the three emergency boxes for this kind of thing,' Bonnie Mae said. 'There's everything and anything you could possibly need in there.'

'I'll go, then,' Meg said, tensing with anticipation. 'Is that agreed?'

'Yes,' Dan said. 'Sorry to put it on you, Meg, when you haven't been up here long, but there's no other way, and we know you can cope. Those coastguard guys are really great; all you will have to do is the strictly medical stuff. Take two of the units of blood from here. We have enough.'

'We're sending a nurse, Wayne,' Bonnie Mae yelled at the intercom. 'You tell them coastguard guys to take good care of her, now! None of the heroics! We'll be ready in ten minutes, at the clinic door. Come and get her!'

'OK, that's great! Greg will be there pronto with the truck. Thanks, you guys! Over and out.' Wayne Keeling's voice clicked off.

'Who does he think he is, with that "over and out"

bit?' Bonnie Mae laughed. 'Well, Meg, come on; I'll help you with the emergency boxes—they weigh a ton each; we'll get them to the clinic door. I'll have to scrub out for a few minutes, Craig.'

Bonnie Mae ripped off her rubber gloves and went to the operating-room door. 'Nuna!' she bawled at the top of her lungs. 'Get the hell in here!' When Nuna appeared as though by magic, she continued, 'You'll have to be the circulating nurse. Just don't touch anything sterile. Be back in a minute. Ready, Meg?'

'Yes. . .I. . .' She hesitated, wanting to say something to Craig as she headed towards the door, more than a simple goodbye. It was impossible. 'I hope Mr Tataniq will be OK.'

'He will be,' Dan said calmly. 'Look after yourself, Meg. Good luck.'

'Meg!' Craig's voice stopped her in her tracks as she had the door open to leave the OR. 'Take care. Don't take any unnecessary risks.' He turned towards her and their eyes met in the few seconds that she paused in the doorway.

'No. . .I won't. Bye.' His words warmed her as she walked away, suddenly nervous now, gearing up for action.

Between the two of them she and Bonnie Mae humped the three heavy emergency boxes as quickly as possible to the clinic door, from where Greg Farley would take over.

'You go over and get dressed, Meg,' Bonnie said then in a brisk manner. 'Put on your warmest gear; you never know what can happen out there. Take the snow-shoes and one of the guns, and a bit of food and drink. Don't forget the ammo. All in ten minutes, eh?' Then she clasped Meg to her in a spontaneous hug. 'You take real good care of yourself, hon! You won't be any good to anyone else if you don't! Sorry you

got dumped with this, but I really am feeling pretty
lousy myself.'

'I'll be OK.' Meg hugged her in return. 'You take
care too.'

'Remember. . .give the injured guys the antihista-
mine and the pain-killers first, then you can go to
work on them. All those syringes are pre-loaded.
Good luck.'

'Thanks, Bonnie. Bye.' Then she ran, going back
along the passage and to the covered way to the
annexe.

In her room she kicked off her shoes and ripped off
the scrub suit. Warm thermal underwear, to cover her
legs and arms, went on over her tights. Then she added
several layers, ending up with the insulated snow-
pants, heavy mukluks and her warmest parka. In the
kitchen she hastily stuffed food into a bag. All at once
she felt very lonely.

Greg Farley was already waiting for her at the clinic
door when she arrived. 'Hi there, Meg. Great to see
you again. . .although maybe different circumstances
would be better, eh? All in a day's work, eh? These
the boxes to go?'

'Yes. These two are dead weights.'

'OK. I'll take those, if you can get the other one.'

It was already dark outside. A blast of chill air
greeted them as they emerged. 'The coastguard guys
are waiting for you at the airstrip with the helicopter,
one of those big machines you see patrolling the Gulf,'
Greg explained in a conversational manner. 'Real
experienced guys, they are. You'll be safe with them.
They'll be keeping in touch with us, then we'll let the
medical station know when you guys will be coming
back with the injured. We're planning to hold any
planes that are headed for Yellowknife, so that we can
ship those guys out if need be. We've also asked for

an air-ambulance to come up from the city, but don't
know if it will get here in time.'

Greg kept up a monologue as they drove to the
airstrip, for which Meg was grateful; he let her know
what she was likely to encounter, how the communi-
cations would work. 'Those mines are pretty
sophisticated,' he went on. 'They have a lot of
entrances, warm offices, good facilities. You can drive
a truck inside. They've still got some power on there,
although they were in the process of shutting the place
down temporarily.'

The helicopter was huge, with twin propellor
systems, back and front. The noise was deafening. The
pilot and two other crew members were very obviously
waiting for her. As the pick-up truck stopped beside
the machine they jumped down to haul up her equipment and to give her a head-set to protect her ears
from noise. In no time at all she was installed in her
seat, with a safety-belt around her middle, having
waved a hasty goodbye to Greg, and the huge machine
was quivering for the lift-off. There would be little
opportunity for conversation. The mine was west and
south of Chalmers Bay; that much she knew
from Greg.

As they rose up over the frozen ground, Meg looked
at the darkened window beside her, seeing only her
own indistinct reflection. An image of chocolate-coated
doughnuts floated incongruously before her mind's
eye, and she heard again the voice of Bonnie Mae
saying, 'You never know when you can get to eat again
in this place!'

CHAPTER TWELVE

'I'D RATHER not take off in this wind unless I really have to; it seems like there's a storm coming up. How bad are those two guys?' The helicopter pilot addressed Meg outside the staff office area in the huge underground cavern that was the main entrance to the Carter Lake mine, where they had come to talk in private, a very hasty conference. From the entrance to the outside, about fifty yards from where they stood, they could hear the wind howling like a hundred demented banshees.

'The one they call Cam,' she said, keeping her voice low. 'He's quite bad. . .a head injury, bleeding inside his skull; something should be done about it soon; he's going to need burr holes drilled in his skull to let out the blood. At the moment I'm more worried about his chest; I think he's got at least one fractured rib which may have perforated his lung on the right side. Anyway, as far as I can tell, he's got blood and air leaking into his chest cavity. He's got to have a chest tube put in quickly. I could do it if I had to; I've got the necessary equipment in the emergency boxes. But I'd rather not. . .'

'What's involved with that?' The pilot squinted at her thoughtfully, weighing up the pros and cons of taking off immediately, now that the basic first aid had been accomplished.

'I'd have to cut through the chest wall, at the side. . .' Meg went on to explain how and why.

'Yeah. . .I get the picture. We're caught between the devil and the deep blue sea.'

172

'I think he's also got a lacerated spleen, which is bleeding too. The right leg's fractured. . .the femur. . .I really think we've got no choice about taking off.' As she uttered the words, she knew that they could crash in high winds too. 'He could bleed to death,' she added. 'The IV blood I've got running in, and the oxygen I'm giving him, will keep him going for a while.' She paused to swallow the remains of a cup of coffee, feeling growing anxiety about the condition of the two men. 'The second one's not as bad, no obvious fractures. . .maybe a slight head injury.'

'Mmm. . .'

'What do you think caused that rock-fall that trapped the two men?' There had been no time before to ask the question which had been burning to be asked. The men had walked into a tunnel along a rail-car track, then there had been a mysterious fall of rock.

'Sabotage, if you ask me. There's some rivalry going on between mine owners, leading to some dirty tricks. The RCMP will sort it out. Ours not to reason why, you know!' The pilot looked at Meg cynically, his lips compressed in a hard line.

'I see. . .' she said.

'OK.' Her companion came to a quick decision. 'We'll go. We'll stay as close to the ground as possible, ready for a quick landing if need be.' He indicated that she should precede him into the cramped office where the two injured men were lying on stretchers on the floor and the other two crew members, plus two workers attached to the mine staff, were keeping an eye on them.

'OK, guys,' the pilot announced. 'Let's move it! We're on our way.'

'Just let me take one more blood-pressure reading before you move them,' Meg said, adjusting the oxygen mask on Cam's face, which was attached to the small, portable oxygen tank that she had brought with her in the emergency kits. Another fear was that the oxygen would run out before they got back to the medical station.

'How are you feeling, Cam?' Bending down close to his face, she spoke to him as she pumped up the blood-pressure cuff attached to his arm at the same time. 'We're going to be moving out now, taking you to the Chalmers Bay medical station.'

Cam closed and opened his eyes weakly, indicating to her that he was all right. The skin of his face had an unhealthy yellowish tinge, his lips bluish. As Meg calmly read his blood-pressure on the gauge, she felt a renewal of her fear, keeping her expression serene as Cam watched her. Without undue hurry she turned up the oxygen level slightly, then increased the flow of the blood that was moving through the intravenous tubing.

'You're going to be fine, Cam.' She smiled at him. 'Just hang in there.' As she straightened up, her eyes met those of the watchful pilot and there was no need for her to tell him, or the others present, that they had to move quickly. They knew their job. Wordlessly, four of them picked up the stretcher on which Cam lay and within minutes were out of the office with it, moving swiftly towards the yawning, dark exit of the mine where the rising storm awaited them.

'I'd like to put a call through to the medical station, if I may?' Meg asked one of the mine workers. 'Then I guess you will contact the RCMP as soon as we're airborne, to let them know we're on our way? I would like the helicopter to land right beside the medical station, not at the airstrip. Can you tell them that, please?'

'Sure can!' The man hurried to make a satellite connection to the medical station for her. In a few moments she heard Craig's voice, somewhat muffled, at the other end of the line.

'Craig?' With the receiver close to her ear, she found herself gabbling, as though she might be cut off any minute. 'We're on our way. Head injury. . . needs burr holes. Chest injury. . .quite bad, I think. Lacerated spleen, I reckon. . .possibly liver as well. Fractured right femur. Multiple bruising and lacerations. That's one of them. The other isn't so bad. . .maybe head injury. We're coming right to you, not to the airstrip. That's it!'

'OK, Meg. We'll be ready for you.' Craig's voice, sounding so normal, warmed her. 'You know how to put in the chest tube if you have to? And how to intubate?'

'Yes, I think so.'

'Don't hesitate if he's turning blue. Hang in there, honey. See you shortly.'

'Bye.' As she hung up, the men returned for the other stretcher, lifting it up with a unified effort.

As they set a brisk pace out of the mine, Meg followed behind with one of the emergency kits, which weighed considerably less now that much of the equipment was in use. The screaming wind snatched at them as they emerged, taking their breath away as they braced themselves against it. Only now could she really understand why the pilot had hesitated. While they had been inside the mine, the enormity of the change in the weather had not been entirely evident. Fear for her own safety now inched its way into her awareness for the first time, so absorbed had she been with the fate of the two men. A wet snow, which swirled around them, stinging their faces, compounded the problem.

The helicopter seemed to wait for them stoically as they hoisted themselves aboard. The interior was designed for emergencies such as this. While Meg settled her equipment, the crew members secured the

two stretchers to the floor and the oxygen equipment
to the side of the spacious main cabin, while the engine
throbbed.

There was a distinct difference in the take-off this
time as the wind buffeted the helicopter, making it
shudder. Meg began her routine of checking the vital
signs of her patients, then she got out the sterile packs
containing everything she would need for the insertion
of the chest tube on Cam, if need be. As she loosened
the clothing around his chest which she had previously
cut at the seams in the first examination, she spoke to
him soothingly, reassuring him. She could tell by listening with her stethoscope how quickly blood was seeping
into his chest cavity.

Never before in her life had she experienced such
intense physical fear as she felt now, as the helicopter
lurched sickeningly, not even during the moments of
claustrophobia that she had experienced in the mine
when she had been required to crawl through a hole
in the fallen rocks to get to her patients; other types
of fear bore no comparison to that associated with
possible imminent annihilation. Get a grip on yourself,
girl! she admonished herself silently, sternly. And get
in that chest tube. . .now!

'I'm going to have to insert a chest tube,' she said
to one of the crew. 'Could you stand by to help me,
if I need it?'

'Sure!' The man was beside her immediately.

As she explained to Cam what she would have to
do, she recalled all the times she had seen a chest tube
being inserted by doctors in the emergency department
at University Hospital. As she opened up the packs of
sterile instruments and gloves, she concentrated on the
sound of Craig's voice saying to her, 'Hang in there,
honey. See you shortly.'

* * *

The powerful helicopter hovered like a great noisy, vibrating bird above the frozen snow near the back entrance of the medical station which had been designed for the purpose to which it was now to be put. Clouds of thin, powdery snow blew up around them as they struggled out after it had touched down, illuminated by the light from the open door of the clinic, where muffled figures waited for them.

Swiftly the stretchers were unfastened from their clamps in the helicopter and passed out through the door. As Meg struggled after them, transferring what was left of the equipment, she saw Craig and Dan, in outdoor clothing, waiting to escort the injured men inside.

'You OK, Meg?' Craig shouted to her above the din of the rotating blades.

'Yes!' There was no time to say more as they all battled the wind to get inside.

Once inside, the two doctors ripped off their outer clothing and left it in a heap, and helped carry the stretchers into the OR. From now on, it would be a concentrated race against time. Meg caught a glimpse of Bonnie Mae already in the room, scrubbed and ready to go, surrounded by tables of sterile drapes and instruments. She too divested herself of her outer gear, put on a scrub suit, and entered the OR. Another operating table had been moved into the room. Silently Meg went to help as the men were positioned on the tables.

'You'll have to scrub too, Meg. We're going to do them both at once,' Bonnie Mae called to her. 'I've got everything ready for you. Sorry, no tea-break, kid!' she added, with a sympathetic smile.

'This place looks as though there's been a whole series of explosions!' Bonnie Mae stood, hands on hips, in

the centre of the disrupted operating-room, which
looked as though every instrument and every sponge
in the place had been used. She laughed at the sight,
almost hysterical with relief now that they could, at
long last, relax. All they had to do now was clear up
the monumental mess. A huge pile of dirty linen took
up a corner; stainless-steel bowls were filled with used
instruments, and the anaesthetic machine and cart
looked as though a mad artist had thrown equipment
around in all directions.

They had done burr holes on Cam to let out the
blood in his skull; they had put in a second chest tube
and done a tracheostomy just in case; then they had
done an abdominal operation on him to repair the
lacerated spleen, deciding not to open the chest. Craig
and Meg had done that together, then they had put
metal plates and screws on the fractured femur. Bonnie
Mae had worked with Dan on their other patient, keeping an eye on the anaesthetics as best they could.

As they had worked, racing against the clock, they
had received word from the airstrip that an air ambulance, ordered hours before from Yellowknife, was
getting close and that the helicopter was still standing
by to take their patients to the airstrip as soon as it
arrived. Several paramedics were with the ambulance.
Even so, they also needed a doctor. Dan had elected
to go on the flight, while Craig had gone with them
to the airstrip.

'Don't mention explosion. . .please!' Meg laughed,
feeling close to mild hysteria herself, and light-headed
with fatigue. 'That appears to be what happened at
the mine.'

'Yeah, well, we did it!' Bonnie said, echoing Meg's
sense of accomplishment and triumph. 'They all made
it! And I think they'll make it to Yellowknife too.
I feel sorry for Dan; he must be just about ready

to drop, even though he said he was so wound up he wouldn't be able to sleep for another day anyway.'

'Yes, but he was right about killing three birds with one stone. . .if you'll excuse the word "killing". . . getting Mr Tataniq shipped out, as well as those two. I'm really glad that Mr Tataniq survived; I wasn't sure that he was going to make it,' Meg said. 'And Cam. . . he was such a mess. . . It seems like a miracle that he's OK.'

'If you hadn't put in that chest tube he might not have been OK,' Bonnie Mae said, ready now to perform a verbal post-mortem on all that had happened. She pulled her surgical mask down from her face so that it dangled around her neck, and she gave Meg a knowing look. 'You were great!'

'I was thinking the same about you. . .everything ready that we could possibly need. . . It all went like clockwork.'

'All in a day's work, hon!' Bonnie Mae said modestly, divesting herself of her blood-spattered surgical gown and tossing it on to the heap in the corner. 'Craig was as worried as hell about you while you were away; he kept looking at the clock and asking Nuna to check with the RCMP to see if they had any news. He got quite irritable at one point, like a bear with a sore head. Then when they told us there was a storm out there, that you were temporarily grounded, I thought he was going to start throwing instruments about the place. We haven't had an instrument-thrower here for some time!'

'Bonnie, you exaggerate,' Meg laughed as she swiftly cleared up.

'I ain't kidding! There's more to him and you than meets the eye.'

'Maybe he was feeling guilty that he didn't go

himself,' Meg commented, an uncontrollable grin stealing across her face.

'Nah. . .' Bonnie Mae said. 'It's more than that. Anyway, he should be back from the airstrip pretty soon; they should be taking off any minute now.'

'Get stuck in, Bonnie Mae!' Meg began to stuff dirty linen into a large canvas laundry bag at a furious pace. 'How come you're so chirpy anyway? I thought you were sick!'

'Yeah, but in this place you have to ignore being sick until you're ready to drop. That's what I'm doing.'

There wasn't much left of the night by the time Meg let herself into the annexe later. Opening the door quietly, she experienced a heavy feeling of expectation, like a sickness.

Craig was waiting for her in the sitting-room, in a chair, his head thrown back, his eyes closed and his long legs stretched out before him. She paused, immobile, when he opened his eyes and got to his feet with one slow, easy movement. Then she could see that he looked totally exhausted; his dark hair fell untidily over his forehead and his shadowed eyes regarded her steadily with an unfathomable expression.

'Would you like a drink, Meg?' he said softly. 'Whisky and soda? Brandy? I brought some with me. You could probably use a drink after what you've been through.'

'Yes, I could. . .just a little brandy. . . Thank you.' She knew she looked equally drained, physically and mentally.

The drink he poured for her was the best French brandy. Naturally. . . Only the best for Craig Russell, she thought wildly; the best of everything. No doubt when he came to choose a wife, if he ever did, he would choose one to match the brandy.

When he came close to her again she felt herself trembling inwardly, unable to look him in the face. They had been through so much together in the past few hours.

'I want to congratulate you,' he said quietly. 'For putting in that chest tube. . .for doing it so well. You did everything right, and you probably saved that guy's life. What you did made my job so much more straightforward.'

She looked at him then, suspecting that perhaps there was a hint of sarcasm in his words, in the light of some of his previous remarks. But the look he gave her was steady, serious, tinged with something that might have been humility.

'Thank you. It didn't come easily, I can assure you, putting in that tube,' she said truthfully, her voice scarcely audible. 'And I guess that's the greatest understatement I've ever made. Will they be all right, do you think?' With a kind of clinical detachment, she noted that her hand was shaking as she reached forward to take the glass from him.

'Provided that nothing happens on the flight—bleeding mainly, or maybe a cardiac arrest with Mr Tataniq—they should be OK. I'm pretty confident they will be,' he said. 'They have enough trained people looking after them, enough equipment.'

'Yes, I think so too. . .I hope so. . .'

'You know all that anyway, I don't have to explain it to you, do I? I've enquired about John Oldman again, by the way. Yesterday, actually. He's doing very well.'

'I'm glad. He was so. . .nice.'

They were fencing, she knew that, stalling for time. She felt like bursting into tears, not knowing quite why, except that she was having some sort of delayed reaction.

'Mmm.' He seemed very aware of her fragile state.

The brandy tasted smooth and potent as she held a sip of it in her mouth, moving it over her tongue before swallowing; it left a pleasant sensation of heat all the way down to her stomach. Neither of them moved away as she slowly emptied her glass.

'I was as worried as hell about you out there,' he said tautly, above her bent head. 'Especially after that storm came up.'

'I was worried too.' She gave a rueful laugh. 'The. . .the pilot didn't want to take off in the wind. . . We had no choice, of course.'

When he took the empty glass from her inert fingers and placed it on the table, she tried to turn away, but found that she could not do it. He put a hand on her shoulder, moving it to touch the skin of her neck above her low-cut scrub suit, stroking, comforting, his own need almost tangible in the air between them. Was the need for her? The cynical thought came to her at the same time as her heart, paradoxically, seemed to melt with love for him and the knowledge that she could meet his need, as well as her own. Would any woman do just as well for his present purposes? The taunting inner voice would not be still.

'All right now?' There was a concerned, tender note in his voice that served to increase her inner turmoil.

'Better,' she said. 'But I think I'm going to collapse.'

Simultaneously they moved, so that his arms engulfed her and she clung to him with desperation, needing his warmth and strength, hearing again in her mind the roar of the helicopter, recalling the terrifying shuddering of the craft as it had been buffeted mercilessly by the wind, then the sight of Cam's waxen face as she had fought to save his life while his blood seeped away.

There had been something boyish and sweet about

Cam, too young to have his life snuffed out by a freak accident. Bravely he had endured his injuries. Somewhere he had a mother, ignorant that her son was then approaching death. At the time she, Meg, had wanted to weep and keen over him, to hold him. Instead she had put in a blood line, splinted and bandaged, eased his pain, reassured him, given him oxygen, then put in a chest tube, working quickly, competently, while the taste of fear had been bitter in her throat. Later, in the operating-room, she had seen the same gritty determination in Craig, Dan and Bonnie Mae as they had laboured over their patients' inert bodies. Now her hopes and prayers were with them and Dan on the long, hazardous flight.

'Oh, Craig. . .hold me,' she said.

They both smelt strongly of betadine, the antiseptic iodine solution that they used to clean their patients' skin prior to operation. Meg didn't care; she pressed her face against Craig's broad chest, shaking with fatigue. Her feet and legs hurt; her whole body ached. For a long time they stood together while he rocked her gently from side to side.

'Come. . .sit down,' he eventually invited her. They sat close together on the sofa, his arm around her protectively as she nestled against him, while he drank his whisky and soda, drawing comfort from each other, each mulling over all that had happened in that hectic day and night. Meg felt as though they had both been mentally stripped down to the bare essentials; what was left was all that really mattered.

When they pulled apart and looked at each other with no pretence, she could see his need of her clearly in his taut features. He put a hand on either side of her face and bent down to kiss her on the mouth, possessively, and she gave herself up to him with no reservations. Their silent communion told her that they were two of a kind, she and Craig. . . Whatever their differences, they were as nothing compared with what they had in common. By the way he held her, rocked her, cupped her tired face with his hands, she knew that he cared; she felt his empathy flow into her, together with his intense desire for her, even as his body heat warmed her. They had both come home.

'I love you, Meg Langham. . .you cute and crazy woman,' he said huskily, his voice shaking with emotion. 'If I didn't want to admit it before, I sure had to admit it today. My biggest fear was that you would be killed out there and I wouldn't have told you I loved you.'

'Craig. . .' she whispered brokenly, hardly daring to believe what she was hearing.

'I had a premonition about you. . .from the moment I saw you. That's why I couldn't believe that you had actually left Gresham. . . Why didn't you wait for me, Meg?'

'When you want something. . .someone. . .so very much——' she searched for the right words '—you're frightened. . .that you can never have it. I ran away. . .before you could reject me. . .'

'I'll never reject you, I couldn't get you out of my mind. I resisted it, of course. . .'

Their lips came together in a long, hungry kiss as they held each other as though they would never be apart again.

'I want to share your bed tonight; I don't want to be alone,' she said unashamedly. 'I had a premonition about you too.' She thought back to the time when she had first seen him, remembering his intense blue eyes looking at her with that self-mocking, cynical expression that told her instantly that he found her attractive. An answering spark had ignited her soul then.

'What am I to you, Meg?'

'I've loved you for a very long time. I want to tell you now, when I feel very sober, very serious, worried, and very, very sad. . .because then you'll know that it's true.' The tears that had been threatening for a long time began to fill her eyes and fall gently down her pale cheeks.

'Yes. . .I know now. I've never felt more sure of anything.' Craig stood up and lifted her to her feet. 'We'll lie down on my bed, keep warm together. I won't be able to sleep until I've heard from Dan. He said he'd call me as soon as they reached the trauma unit in Yellowknife. We've got a long wait.'

'Craig. . .what about Gail?'

'What about her? Gail has never been more than a very good friend. . . Darling, believe me.' Craig held her close, looking down into her upturned face.

'You do have a lot in common,' she persisted softly.

'Yes. . .mainly from our mutual past; we went to school together. It's not the same as what I have with you. I'll always be grateful to Gail for what she's done for me and Rob. . .and for Sonia. But it's you I love, Meg.'

She believed him.

Under a warm quilt they lay in each other's arms, not bothering to undress. A bedside lamp cast a warm orange glow. The brandy that Meg had drunk was beginning to have an effect; she felt a peace stealing over her.

'How about a story?' Craig said, his warm breath close to her ear. 'About you and me, and that ends happily ever after. Mmm?' When he kissed her she could taste her own salty tears on his lips. 'Since that's the only type of story you know. . .and it would be very appropriate for us, don't you think?'

'Are you teasing me?'

'No.'

'What I feel for you is a kind of madness. . .I love you so much. Tell me the story tomorrow. . .just give me the happily ever after now.' She smiled at him, recovering, responding to his kisses, which held a promise for the future. Something miraculous was happening, something she had hardly dared to hope for. . .all the more so because it had happened spontaneously; neither one of them had planned it. Something fragile, yet strong at the same time, trembled between them as they regarded each other in a new-found honesty and trust.

'You're the first woman I've ever really loved,' he said, caressing her cheek with his lips. 'I want to have a wedding song just for us, my darling. This time it will be for real. . .if you will agree?'

'Yes.' She smiled at Craig as the dark ghosts which had seemed to gather around her in the helicopter as she had used all her expertise to save Cam's life, which had waited to claim one of their own, receded and disappeared.

'Are you willing to be a mother to my son? Because he's part of me. . .he's going to be with me for a long time.'

'Yes. I already love him like a mother. . .a real mother. I know he's part of you,' she said, tracing the outline of his mouth with her fingers as he lay on his side next to her, glorying in their mutual feeling of belonging. 'I know you belong together.'

They lay cocooned in the warmth of the fragile building that sheltered them against the blowing snow and cold, waiting for the telephone call that would come from hundreds of miles to the south, to tell them that all was well. As they waited they would become one in mind and body, knowing that it would be forever. They would not be able to sleep, yet as they waited they would both remember the haunting strains of the wedding song, and the words that promised them that the light of their love would be their sun until the spring came again to the north.

MILLS & BOON

Always & Forever

This summer Mills & Boon presents the wedding book of the year—three new full-length wedding romances in one heartwarming volume.

Featuring top selling authors:

Debbie Macomber ♥ Jasmine Cresswell
Bethany Campbell

The perfect summer read!

Available: June 1995   Price: £4.99

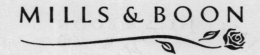

MILLS & BOON

LOVE CALL

The books for enjoyment this month are:

IMPOSSIBLE SECRET   Margaret Barker
A PRACTICE MADE PERFECT   Jean Evans
WEDDING SONG   Rebecca Lang
THE DECIDING FACTOR   Laura MacDonald

———————— ❧ ————————

Treats in store!

Watch next month for the following absorbing stories:

LOVE WITHOUT MEASURE   Caroline Anderson
VERSATILE VET   Mary Bowring
TARRANT'S PRACTICE   Abigail Gordon
DOCTOR'S HONOUR   Marion Lennox

Available from W.H. Smith, John Menzies, Volume One, Forbuoys,
Martins, Tesco, Asda, Safeway and other paperback stockists.

Readers in South Africa - write to:
IBS, Private Bag X3010, Randburg 2125.

SPRING FLOWER COMPETITION

How would you like a years supply of Temptation books ABSOLUTELY FREE? Well, you can win them all! All you have to do is complete the word puzzle below and send it in to us by 31st December 1995. The first 5 correct entries picked out of the bag after that date will win a years supply of Temptation books (*four books every month - worth over £90*). What could be easier?

L	L	E	B	E	U	L	B	Q
P	R	I	M	R	O	S	E	A
I	D	O	D	Y	U	I	P	R
L	O	X	G	O	R	S	E	Y
S	T	H	R	I	F	T	M	S
W	P	I	L	U	T	F	K	I
O	E	N	O	M	E	N	A	A
C	H	O	N	E	S	T	Y	D

COWSLIP

BLUEBELL

PRIMROSE

DAFFODIL

ANEMONE

DAISY

GORSE

TULIP

HONESTY

THRIFT

PLEASE TURN OVER
FOR DETAILS OF HOW
TO ENTER

HOW TO ENTER

Hidden in the grid are various British flowers that bloom in the Spring. You'll find the list next to the word puzzle overleaf and they can be read backwards, forwards, up, down, or diagonally. When you find a word, circle it or put a line through it.

After you have completed your word search, don't forget to fill in your name and address in the space provided and pop this page in an envelope (you don't need a stamp) and post it today. Hurry - competition ends 31st December 1995.

Mills & Boon Spring Flower Competition,
FREEPOST,
P.O. Box 344,
Croydon,
Surrey. CR9 9EL

Are you a Reader Service Subscriber?   Yes ❑   No ❑

Ms/Mrs/Miss/Mr _____

Address _____

_____

_____ Postcode _____

One application per household.   F

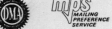

COMP395